GORDON
DANGER A˙

GORDON MEYRICK lived from 1909 to 1943. He was one of eight children. His mother, Kate Meyrick, was a notorious night-club owner between the first and second world wars in London.

He was the author of four crime novels, published between 1941 and 1943, in addition to earlier stage successes. In 1943 Meyrick fell from an upper floor window to his death – the exact circumstances of this tragedy remain unknown.

Dean Street Press have republished two of his classic mysteries: *The Body on the Pavement* and *Danger at my Heels*.

GORDON MEYRICK

DANGER AT MY HEELS

With an introduction by Curtis Evans

DEAN STREET PRESS

INTRODUCTION

GORDON MEYRICK'S corpus of crime fiction appeared in the few short years between 1941 and 1943, the year of his tragic untimely demise at the age of 34. While the book for which he is best known is his posthumously published *The Ghost Hunters* (1947), a collection of short stories about the exploits of Arnold Perry, a most percipient paranormal investigator, which the author completed shortly before his death (though it was not published until four years later), his entertaining crime novels--*The Green Phantom*, *The Body on the Pavement*, *Pennyworth of Murder,* and *Danger at My Heels*--merit reprinting. Decidedly in the thriller vein, Meyrick's mysteries concern gangs of crooks and master criminals in the style of such masters of the form as Edgar Wallace, John Buchan and E. Phillips Oppenheim. This milieu was one with which Meyrick had at least passing acquaintance, for he was the tall, dapper son of Kate Meyrick, England's notorious between-the-wars "Queen of the Nightclubs" and one of the country's most notable cultural figures in the two decades between the First and Second World Wars.

Kate Meyrick was born Kate Evelyn Nason in Ireland in 1875. Having lost her birth parents by the age of seven, Kate with her sister was sent to live with a grandmother and two great-aunts in a sprawling mansion in Dublin (now a five-star Radisson hotel). "Here everything was of a bygone age," she later dryly recalled. "There were three servants who had been in the family for more than half a century, the gardener was eighty-four, the coachman only a year or two his junior. The governesses set to educate my sister and myself were also of an age to harmonise with the surroundings."

To the disappointment of her relations, Kate rejected matrimony with a wealthy man in order to wed a young doctor, Ferdinand Richard Holmes Merrick. After their marriage in 1899 the couple moved to southern England, residing successively at Southsea and Brighton. There Dr. Meyrick, as he now styled himself (this spelling of the surname struck the young couple as posher) treated a clientele of well-off mental patients. Kate meanwhile bore eight children, six daughters and two sons, during the years of her marriage. These were Mary Ethel Isobel (1900-1938), Dorothy Evelyn (1902-1987), Henry Lyster (1903-1968), Kathleen Holmes (1907-1978), Gordon Holmes (1909-1943), Eileen Margaret Nason (1910-1959), Lilian Agnes (1912-1987) and Gwendoline Irene (1914-2002).

Kate's marriage, which had long been troubled, finally broke down irretrievably after the First World War, when she sued Ferdinand for divorce and he counter-sued her, damningly citing a co-respondent. With this standoff achieved, no divorce actually materialized; yet the couple permanently separated, with Kate being left custody of the minor children, including younger son Gordon, who was only ten at the time. Now in her forties, Kate moved with her brood to London and launched a colorful midlife career as a nightclub proprietor. (The partner in her first venture was the man who had been named as the co-respondent in Dr. Merrick's divorce suit.) The middle-aged mother of eight soon became a fixture of city nightlife, as well as, in the stern eyes of legal authority, "the most inveterate lawbreaker in London"—all on account of her grave crime of selling liquor after hours.

The nature of London nightlife had greatly changed after the Great War, as hard-pressed aristocrats sold their regal townhouses, which had become much too expensive to maintain. As one authority has put it, the venue for posh entertaining in the city shifted "from private ballrooms to public nightclubs." For example, Grosvenor House, the splendid townhouse of the Dukes of Westminster, was sold and demolished in 1927 and replaced by a grand hotel (named, appropriately enough, the Grosvenor House Hotel). Detective novelist E.R. Punshon (reprinted by Dean Street Press) referenced the decline of London townhouses in his 1936 novel *The Bath Mysteries*, where we learn that police sergeant Bobby Owen's aristocratic uncle is saddled with a monstrous white elephant of a dilapidated city mansion.

While flagging aristocrats fled from their townhouses, the energetic "Ma Meyrick" (as she was familiarly known to society) stuck her finger into many a boozy pie. Her most famous--or infamous in the eyes of the law--establishment was the "43," so named for its location in the basement at 43 Gerrard Street, Soho. In his novel *Brideshead Revisited*, author Evelyn Waugh referenced both Kate Meyrick and 43, slightly disguised as "Ma Mayfield" and the

"Old Hundredth." Additionally, the detective novelist A. Fielding must have had an approximation of Kate in mind when in her mystery *The Case of the Two Pearl Necklaces* (1936) she devised the character of a notorious female nightclub proprietor, "Mrs. Finch," who is determined to have her daughter, Violet, marry into the aristocracy. Quite contrastingly with Ma Meyrick, however, Fielding's crass and mercenary Mrs. Finch is singularly charmless.

Unfortunately for Kate, her popularity in the City attracted an empowered legal nemesis in the stern form of Sir William Joynson-Hicks, home secretary in the Conservative government of Prime Minister Stanley Baldwin. After taking office Joynson-Hicks vowed "to stamp out the evil of drinking after hours." Under wartime Great Britain's Defence of the Realm Act [DORA], passed in 1914, the government possessed, an authority has noted, "extraordinary powers of interference in public events and private lives." Originally DORA was justified "as a measure to keep munition workers out of the pubs during factory hours," but it was retained in place even after its original justification had vanished. By the end of 1928 the vigilant Sir William had prosecuted sixty-five clubs, including Kate Meyrick's 43.

Kate's legal troubles culminated in her being charged in 1928 with bribing a police sergeant to warn her when her premises were being surveilled. For committing the crime of bribery (which for the remainder of her life she vociferously denied), Kate was sentenced in January 1929 to fifteen months hard labor at Holloway Prison. After her release in

1930 (the year Dorothy L. Sayers's fictional mystery writer Harriet Vane, on trial for murder, was locked up in Holloway in the detective novel *Strong Poison*), the bloodied but unbowed Kate, undeterred from her vocational ways, would serve two briefer stints of incarceration. Increasingly frail after her myriad legal battles and terms of imprisonment, Kate succumbed in an influenza pandemic in 1933. At the time of her death she was only 57.

The censorious Joynson-Hicks had expected to find London's nightclubs "filled with whores" but instead discovered, to his consternation, that they were "crammed with 'society.'" Kate herself was a "lady" who made a great deal of money as a nightclub owner (though she had very little of it left at her death). This lucre she spent lavishly to educate her eight children at elite schools (Rodean and Harrow). Three of her daughters married aristocrats: "May," the 14th Earl of Kinnoull; "Dolly," the 26th Baron de Clifford; and Gwendoline, the youngest, the 6th Earl of Craven. Another daughter, Nancy, wed wealthy Edward FitzRoy St. Aubyn, a kinsman of Baron St. Levan.

Gordon, who unlike his siblings never married, trained as a solicitor, like his elder brother Henry, but in 1935, two years after his mother died, he scored a success on stage at London's Q. Theater with the mystery thriller *The Green Phantom*. Two years later he followed *Phantom* was another criminous Q. Theatre production, *The Second Shot*. After his thirtieth birthday he turned to crime fiction writing as a full-time avocation. Throughout the 1930s Gordon resided with his unmarried sisters on Marylebone Road at

3 Park Square West, part of an elegant row of stuc-
coed Regency houses designed by famed architect
John Nash and completed in 1824. (Before her death
Kate Meyrick had lived there too.) By 1941, however, he was living on his own in tony Kensington at
16e Kensington Court, in a flat in a charming nookish
Victorian-era structure modestly tucked beneath its
taller neighbors. (A one-bedroom flat in this building
recently was offered for sale for one and a quarter million pounds.) It may have been at Kensington Court
that Gordon mysteriously fell from a window to his
death on the pavement in November 1943. A modern
relation of Gordon observes, "whether he threw himself or fell purely by accident or because he was drunk
is unknown." Of course as an inveterate reader of detective novels, when I first read of Gordon's death I
thought not merely of accident or suicide, but also of
murder. In an odd coincidence (or was it?), Gordon's
second detective novel, *The Body on the Pavement*
(originally published in 1942, not too long before
Gordon's death), concerns, as the title suggests, the
mysterious death of a man who falls from--or is he
pushed?--the roof of a posh block of flats.

Thus in *The Body on the Pavement* is another
strange murder case presented to ace Scotland Yard
detective Rex Haig, who is handsome, expensively
educated, relentlessly humorous and rather smug.
(Whether the humor or the smugness wins out will
depend on the reader.) Perhaps reflecting the author's own social insecurities--Gordon was educated
at Harrow, but his doting mama naturally had a notorious reputation as a nightclub owner arrested sev-

eral times for selling liquor after hours in violation of DORA--many of the characters in the novel (Rex of course excepted) seem to be consumed with public school envy.

It soon becomes apparent to the reader that *The Body on the Pavement* is less a tale of austere detection than a breezy mystery thriller in the manner of the late bestselling English Crime King Edgar Wallace. In the classic Wallace manner, Inspector Haig realizes he is up against a dastardly conspiracy by a criminal gang. To entertain his readers Gordon presents a colorful and frequently quirky cast of characters, including pretty Joan Hamilton, imperiled country heiress; a small-time con named (distractingly for modern American readers) Larry King; a handsome crooked couple, representatives of "the more dubious section of London's West End population," Tony Miller and Millicent Thorpe ("And don't call me Millicent. The name is Thelma."); Oscar Pendleton, a pansyish bachelor ("I was sitting in that chair. . . . reading a book by Marcel Proust."); and Mr. Mander, a prim lawyer with a passion for peroxide blondes. These characters, as well as the author's rapid pace and lightly humorous writing style, elevate *The Body on the Pavement* above the usual period British thriller. These same qualities are present as well in Gordon's *Danger at My Heels*, rather a pastiche of John Buchan's classic thriller *The Thirty-Nine Steps* (1915). *Danger* also benefits from its wartime detail (the London Blitz) and the author's obvious familiarity with London.

Why did Gordon, a single man in his early thirties, apparently not serve in the Second World War? I have no definite answers, though one can make surmises. In *Danger*, which is set in the spring of 1941, Michael Stephen, the narrator of the novel, who is the age of the author at the time the novel takes place, has returned to England after eight years in a foreign country, with the hope of serving in the navy. Certainly aspects of the novel must have been drawn from Gordon's life:

> I . . . found there was a good chance for the R.N.V.R. [Royal Naval Volunteer Reserve]— only it meant a wait of two or three months. So I took a quarterly tenancy of a flat in Kensington Court, on the top floor, and went into immediate possession.
>
> At Kensington Town Hall I got a gas-mask, and from the Food Office a ration card; this entitled me to a quarter of a pound of butter, half a pound of sugar, two ounces of tea, and one and tuppence worth of meat a week. I dumped this lot in my new flat, and went out to get some lunch. I remember worrying lest a period of boredom and inactivity lay before me. It makes me smile to think of that now.

At the local pub the narrator, in rather an amazing coincidence (this sort of thing happens in John Buchan too, not to mention Edgar Wallace), is taken for a near double of his, someone who had an appointment at the pub at the very same time. And of course this near double is up to no good at all. Soon not only the police, but enemy spies, are after our hero. The only thing for him to do is, to quote the title of a Patricia Wentworth thriller, *Run!*

As mentioned at the top of this introduction, Gordon Meyrick wrote two other crime novels, *The Green Phantom* (an Edgar Wallace title if ever there were one) and *Pennyworth of Murder*, both of which it would be jolly to see reprinted, both for their intrinsic entertainment value and as testaments to a tragically foreshortened life of promise left unfulfilled. One cannot help but feel that the Meyricks, mother and son, got rather a raw deal from life. When he died at 34 after publishing his four crime novels Gordon Meyrick left an estate of just £131 (today about £5300, or USD7100), which he loyally left to his elder brother Henry—a pennyworth of murder indeed! Today Gordon lies forgotten in a humble plot in Kensal Green cemetery in the Royal Borough of Kensington and Chelsea, rather overgrown with grass, together with his beloved mother, Kate, the deposed Queen of the Nightclubs. If Edgar Wallace was the King of Thrillers and E. Phillips Oppenheim the Prince of Storytellers, perhaps we can at least posthumously crown Gordon Meyrick one of the genre's royal princelings.

Curtis Evans

To

PENNY

*In gratitude for her help in
this adventure*

CHAPTER I

IN MARCH, 1941, the S.S. *Cawnstor*, bound for England, was bombed off the south-west coast and sank quickly. I was lucky enough to be picked up by a destroyer that got us ashore at Swansea. My papers and passport were in the sea, but my money, tied in a belt round my middle, was safe.

I had been out of the country for eight years, so it was worth a wetting to get back. As soon as the formalities were over, I went to London, because that was the place I wanted most to see. Probably many people think of that city as dirty and unfriendly—but to me it's home. I knew as soon as I smelt it at Paddington Station that I was back for good.

When you're away, imagination can play hell with you. I had pictured an England torn and stressed by bombing; instead, it was extraordinary to see how small was the damage—relatively speaking, I mean.

Most of the features of a modern city at war were new to me; the sandbags on doorsteps, the water tanks in the street, the air-raid shelters, windows criss-crossed with paper to prevent splinters flying; the curiosity of blast-glass windows, intact in the shell of a bombed house, or a bath dangling, apparently unsupported, in the air. And overhead the balloon barrage—silver sausages floating in a misty blue.

The most extraordinary thing was the calmness of the people. Later I learnt that after a bad blitz there was considerable tension. Then, with glass and debris littering the streets, tired A.R.P. and A.F.S. workers dealt with blitzed and burning houses, while grim silent crowds watched; the dust and smoke hung in the air—you could smell the air raid for days.

London seemed more silent than I remembered it. Like a convalescent invalid, she had taken a few knocks, and now, with her wounds patched up, she was out and about again.

I spent that evening at the Ritz Cinema, seeing *Gone With The Wind*. Afterwards, there came my first experience of another phenomenon—the black-out. To me—a novice—it was uncanny. A giant city sheltering in the cloak of night; most of its inhabitants burrowed underground. I have a vivid peace-time memory of Piccadilly Circus. The electric light signs flashing at the corner of Shaftesbury Avenue and over the Monico; the brilliantly-lit facade of the London Pavilion and the Criterion. Crowds, noise, cars, evening dress. Now, nothing but a black void. Pin-points of light from slowly moving cars, ghostly omnibuses; dimly-seen pedestrians, a few of whom flashed dimmed torches. . . . Uncertain steps—and a gingerly feeling for the edge of pavements. The night presses on you; gone is the sense of direction and distance, a hundred yards can seem like a mile. I was glad to get back to my hotel and from the bedroom window watch my first air raid. The barrage was terrific; roar after roar of anti-aircraft guns. Each blast shook the house, and the sound went reverberating over the roof-tops like thunder. The momentary flash, lighting the buildings in silhouette, gave you the impression of lightning. Away in the south-east a red glow lit the heavens. Incendiary bombs had started some fires.

Then there appeared half a dozen star-like objects that hung suspended in the sky. These parachute flares gave a white, dazzling effect, lending their immediate vicinity the appearance of ghost-like day. Occasionally there was a sickening crump as a bomb fell.

It was an exhilarating scene. Though it made me feel small and helpless—and very angry. I wished that I had a giant hand to haul down those murderous insects that were indiscriminately bombing the civilians of London.

The gun-fire was noisy; though, curiously enough, the most persistent sound and the one you noticed above everything else was the noise of enemy aeroplanes; these sounded as if they were exactly above your head. It took me some time to get to sleep, though I was lucky enough, at that, for it was the last night of comparative peace that I was to know for some time. The next day things started to happen—as far as I was concerned, I mean. But I'll come to that in a moment.

I ought to explain that I was back to get into the Navy. Try to, that is. My age group—the thirty-two's—had long since been conscripted, and I had a nasty feeling that they might now leave you no choice of service. However, I saw a fellow at the Admiralty, and then at Rex House, and found there was a good chance for the R.N.V.R.—only it meant a wait of two or three months. So I took a quarterly tenancy of a flat in Kensington Court, on the top floor, and went into immediate possession.

At Kensington Town Hall I got a gas-mask, and from the Food Office a ration card; this entitled me to a quarter of a pound of butter, half a pound of sugar, two ounces of tea, and one and tuppence worth of meat a week. I dumped this lot in my new flat, and went out to get some lunch. I remember worrying lest a period of boredom and inactivity lay before me. It makes me smile to think of that now.

I bought an *Evening Standard* and turned into a pub in the Kensington High Street. One side of the room was partitioned off with wooden cubicles. As I came abreast the first of these, a curious thing happened. A man got to his feet and said, "Hullo, you're early!"

Then he stopped—very suddenly.

He was a small, ordinary-looking fellow, wearing a raincoat. He had a thin, pinched face—and there was nothing remarkable about him except perhaps his eyes; these were blue and deep-set, and gave him a look of cunning. He was gaping in surprise. I could not imagine what had startled him! Certainly I had never seen him before in my life.

"Sorry," he muttered, "I thought you were someone else."

He sank back in his seat, and I went on to an empty cubicle.

When I had given my order to a waiter, I opened the newspaper.

We had raided the Lofoten Isles. . . . Eden, the Foreign Secretary, had left Greece after discussions with Greek leaders. . . . Weather reports were forbidden, but the paper gave an account of the conditions over the Straits of Dover; a reminder of the possibility of a Nazi invasion.

I glanced down the amusement column. John Gielgud was in Barrie's *Dear Brutus* at the Globe Theatre, and there was *Applesauce* at the Palladium with Max Miller. The Piccadilly Hotel and the Lansdowne Restaurant both advertised dancing thirty feet below ground level. "Eat in safety." I wondered what future generations would think of notices such as these.

On the wall was pinned the reproduction of a drawing by "Fougasse," a warning against careless talk. It represented Hitler leaning out from under a table and listening intently to two gentlemen. My mind turned to spies and spying. I wondered how many had got in with the refugees from Germany and Austria, and whether our supervision was strict enough.

Soon I finished and went out. As I turned down the High Street, someone touched me on the arm. Two men had followed me out of the pub.

They were in the middle forties. One was fat and round of face, dressed in a cheviot overcoat. The other was thin with a dark jowl. Both their faces were grave. I think if you had asked me to guess their occupations, I would have said that they were builders or some sort of artisans who had gone to the public-house for their midday beer and sandwich.

The fat one said, "I think your name is Carr."

I shook my head.

"No—Stephen."

The face of the fat man hardened; a purposeful look appeared in his eyes.

"I think not, Mr. Carr. I am Detective-Inspector Cartwright" (I think he said of the Special Branch), "and I must ask you to come with us."

I was amazed.

"But why?"

"You will be charged under the Official Secrets Act, and under the Defence Regulations."

"Nonsense!" I said, smiling. "Look here, unless this is a joke, you've got me mixed up with someone else. My name is Michael Stephen—really!"

"We don't want any trouble. You'd better come quietly."

They moved closer. The thin one had one of his hands in his pocket; and I knew, as clearly as if I could see it, that he was handling an automatic.

It all seemed rather unreal. People were passing close to us on the pavement, and the traffic was moving smoothly along the Kensington High Street, that sedate shopping centre; a pretty girl in slacks went by and glanced enquiringly at me. I wondered if she thought we were three men who, after meeting for a drink, were about to go their respective ways.

I could not take the men seriously.

"I don't know what it's all about," I said, "but I think we can clear this up."

"All right," said the fat one, "come along."

He hailed a passing taxi. I do not like being told what to do, and nearly said so. Then I reflected that, if they were really detectives and had made a mistake, it was up to me to help them.

The thin one told the driver to go to Scotland Yard. I asked them what it was all about. Cartwright (the fat one) said, "You'd better wait."

We drove in silence. I was still puffing at my pipe. My mind was not unduly disturbed, though I realized that this would be a nuisance. There would be the business of establishing my identity. Soon we drove through a gateway into a courtyard. The taxi was paid off and I was hurried along a passage into a room. Here were some chairs and a teak table. The walls were bare, the windows barred.

The thin man disappeared, and after a while a slight, grey-haired man came in. He was accompanied by a police stenographer.

"Well, Mr. Carr," he said, "we've had quite a hunt for you. I hope you're not going to give us any trouble."

"On the contrary, I came here to help you," I replied. "There has evidently been a mistake. My name is not Carr."

The elder man shrugged his shoulders.

"We will not quarrel about a name!" He turned to Cartwright. "Have you that photograph?"

The Inspector carried some papers, and from these he took a photograph. He gave this to his superior, who in turn handed it to me.

"Do you deny that that is your photograph?"

The photograph looked as though it had been enlarged from an amateur's snapshot. I do not think that the average man (unlike a woman) knows his face really well. But the sight of these reproduced features surprised me. There was my black hair, my fairly square jaw, and slightly aquiline nose. The lips were, perhaps, fuller than mine, the face fatter and the eyes more closely set. But certainly the general effect was amazingly like myself.

I gave it back.

"Yes, it's certainly like me. But it doesn't happen to be me."

"I don't think lying's going to help you."

It was an excusable case of mistaken identity. It should not take long to put right, and I gave an easy laugh.

"If I tell you about myself, that should clear this up."

"That is what we wish to hear."

I told them my name was Michael Stephen. I gave them details of the bombed S.S. *Cawnstor* and of my movements since. I asked them to ring up the estate agent to verify my address.

"If you don't believe me," I finished, "get in touch with Swansea or the destroyer that put us ashore."

They were looking at me closely, suspiciously.

"We don't deny that you may have done all these things," said the grey-haired man in his soft voice, "but you're still the man we want."

"Who do you think I am?" I burst out.

The older man regarded me unperturbed.

"Will it save time if I tell you that we know of your interest in the Admiralty affair?"

Sudden realization came to me. They thought I was some sort of a spy. I nearly laughed; it was so ridiculous.

"Look here, if you think I'm some sort of spy, you've got to forget it—quickly. Because the man you really want will be getting away."

"But you admit trying to get into the Navy?"

"Of course! Why not?"

"And you've applied for mine-sweeping work!"

"Yes. But you're still making a mistake."

The grey-haired man sighed.

"You know perfectly well what we want. We'll soon find out if you've got it."

He whispered something to Cartwright, who nodded and left the room. I protested, but neither of the men said anything. Finally I fell into a savage silence, and took out my pipe. At the sight of it the grey-haired man said:

"I see you no longer smoke your Pagani black cigars!"

"I've never even heard of Pagani black cigars," I snapped.

"Wise of you to drop your known habits when someone's looking for you."

Soon the Inspector returned, ushering another man into the room. The newcomer was about thirty, with a pale face and restless eyes. He continuously clenched and unclenched his fingers. He was obviously a badly frightened man.

"You see, we got Fergusson," said the grey-haired man.

"I don't know who he is."

"Very well. We'll have another talk, later."

They all went out, leaving me alone. Then Cartwright returned and took me to another room. Here they made me strip to the skin and searched both myself and my clothes. Then they weighed me, photographed me (full face and profile), and took particulars, such as the colour of my eyes and hair. Finally they took my finger-prints.

I had a few angry things to say and said them. Eventually I ended up back in the first room.

I sat there alone for about an hour, working up a beautiful temper. I got too heated to worry about my position, though I realized that without papers (mine were in the sea) and without a soul in England who really knew me, it would be difficult proving my identity, at any rate, for some time.

I was just about as cross as a man can be, when the grey-haired man came in and at one stroke punctured my inflated rage. He crawled; he apologized all ways he knew how. There had been a terrible mistake, and he could only throw himself on my mercy. Particulars they had just taken about me did not check up with those of the man they wanted. They had telephoned Swansea, and my trip abroad made it certain that I could not be Carr.

Would I accept his apology? Was there anything he could do to put it right? Above all, would I be good enough to say nothing of what had happened. Something big was at stake. He did not want the man they really sought to be warned.

There was nothing I could do but say all right, and accept their offer to be taken home in a taxi.

In the cab I pulled at my pipe. It was annoying to have lost the best part of an afternoon (I had been arrested about one, and it was now four o'clock). Against that, it would make a good story. I dismissed the whole thing from my mind—including a little nagging worry that something was wrong somewhere.

Then occurred an incident that should have made me suspicious. I stopped at the Overseas Club, and when I came out my taxi was still waiting.

"Paid for to Kensington Court," said the driver.

I thought this very considerate of the Metropolitan Police.

We rattled to a stop in Kensington Court, and I went upstairs to my flat; on a landing were buckets and a stirrup pump (the householders' indispensable requisites with which to fight that modern pest—the incendiary bomb.)

The estate agent had told me that it was customary (and sometimes compulsory) to form fire-fighting groups amongst the houses. The suburban dweller, when he lent over his neighbour's fence, now courteously borrowed, not the garden roller, but a stirrup pump, "As a fire has dropped into one of the bedrooms, old boy."

I went into the kitchen to make myself a cup of tea. As I sat waiting for the water to boil, that uneasy, nagging worry came back.

Something *was* wrong somewhere. The Scotland Yard business did not add up right. When I first got there they were certain that I was the right man. They had questioned me, and produced that fellow—what was his name?—Fergusson (whoever he might be). It was only afterwards that they had taken my particulars. Surely, if there had been any doubt, they would have checked particulars straight away.

Suddenly I gave a gasp. Something had become very clear. Inspector Cartwright and the dark-jowled detective had not been in the public-house by chance. They were there because they expected to find Carr.

The fellow in the raincoat who had spoken to me. He fell neatly into the picture. What was that he had said? "Hullo, you're early—"; and then, "Sorry, I thought you were someone else."

Of course! He thought I was Carr—*because he was waiting for him.*

The police knew that Carr was going to meet some-one in the public-house; but, presumably, they did not know whom. By one shot in a million I, who hap-pened to look something like the wanted man, had walked in. The detectives had waited, hoping my con-federate would turn up, but when I went out alone they arrested me.

They had let me go because they expected me to lead them to someone—or something; whatever it was they had searched me for at Scotland Yard.

I went into the living-room and looked round. It was difficult to tell if anything had been disturbed. Indeed, I would not have known, but for a knot on one of the parcels. It had been loose and I had retied it. Since then it had been undone and then done up again.

The flat had been searched in my absence.

On an impulse I looked out of the window, being careful not to be seen myself. Below was the square and beyond the park. . . . A few seconds later and I would have missed him. On the steps, talking to a man, was the dark-jowled detective. He stayed but a few seconds. Then, turning, he hurried away. His companion went down the area steps into the house.

They still thought I was Carr and were waiting for me.

A hiss of escaping steam came from the kitchen. Mechanically I made a pot of tea.

I tried to recall what the grey-haired man had said at Scotland Yard. He had made a point that I could have done all the things I claimed to have done, and yet still be Carr. This suggested that, beyond the photograph, the police knew very little about that individual. Their lack of knowledge made it awkward, for no one knew me well in England.

I sat very still, automatically drinking the milkless tea, listlessly crumbling a piece of cake.

A hush, like a tangible thing, hung over the flat. Suddenly I hated it; the place had become a prison. Outside, they were waiting for me; ready to arrest me. It was only a question of time. When they had me—what then? There would be a period of restraint while I sought to convince them. But supposing this was not possible? What if they believed to the end that I was Carr?

I thought of him, somewhere in London, working against England. Burrowing like a mole while he helped to undermine her. When they took me they would think they had him. He would be free to continue his work. Then I knew that I must find Carr. It might be the only way to convince them. More important, it might be the one way to stop him.

My brain, which had clouded, came to life. I felt resourceful; ready for escape. Going into the living-room, I pulled out my pipe. It would have to be carefully thought out—this escape of mine. Outside, the net was drawn pretty tight. I was up against men trained to man-hunt.

I turned a few ideas over in my mind. My first thoughts centred round something in the nature of a dash for freedom. Only that line of country was hopeless. Something more subtle was necessary.

I tried putting myself in their place. What would their instructions be? How much rope would I be allowed?

It was clear that they would not give me much of a run. If I went out in daylight no doubt I could wander about, for they could follow me. But once the blackout came—then, surely, they would act. They could not risk my slipping off in the dark. Nevertheless, it was for night that I must wait. It was my only ally.

Then an idea suggested itself. They expected me to contact somebody. As long as they thought I was leading them somewhere, then just so long would they let me go free. Anyway, that was my guess.

It so happened that the telephone was still connected. The last occupant had left, like so many Londoners, in a hurry. Now, if the police were as smart as I hoped they were, they would expect me to use the telephone, and might have a man listening in.

I looked up the Piccadilly Hotel, and asked for Major Maxim Buckley. I chose that name because, to the best of my knowledge, no such person existed.

They, naturally, told me they had never heard of him.

I affected surprise, and paused as if in thought.

"Apparently he hasn't arrived yet," I said. "But I want to leave a message for him. Will you tell him, when he arrives, that Mr. Stephen wants to see him very urgently to-night. I'll meet him in the cocktail bar at eight forty-five. And on no account is he to go out. Tell him not to bother to ring me; but he must wait. Have you got that?"

I made my voice sound pretty urgent, and repeated everything twice. I acted like a desperate man. If any policeman was listening in, he should have been duly impressed.

Well, there it was. If they had heard me, I might have a chance to get away; and if they hadn't, then it probably meant a cell for that night.

I had to decide what to take with me. My hat and coat, obviously. Apart from that and the clothes I stood up in—nothing else. There was sufficient money in my belt for some considerable time. So there was no need for anxiety on that score.

Food would be useful; and I made some paste sandwiches. There was consolation in being able to use a week's ration of butter in one grand burst. Wrapping the sandwiches and some cake into a parcel, I stowed this into my overcoat pocket.

Then back to the living-room to wait until about eight-thirty. Sitting there, thinking of this strange new London, made the time pass quickly.

Black-out was round about seven-twenty; and at fifteen minutes past I pulled the curtains. Metal shades over the electric lights threw the beam downwards. For in this London of 1941 a glimmer of escaping light would mean a visit from the Warden; it could also invite a sudden oblivion from a falling bomb.

Round about eight came a familiar wail. The sirens were sounding. A nearby gun opened up, and the echo went reverberating through the buildings. No sooner had this died down, then another started. Soon the barrage was going strong. Boom! Boom! A tinkle, like glass, as shrapnel hit the roof above my head. . . . A silence. Then they started again. Soon there came the drone of enemy planes. The curious thing is that you do not feel afraid. Though I hated the shut-in feeling; the dimmed light, the thick curtains pressing against you.

There was a lull in the firing as the first wave of Jerries passed. But soon it started again. Some bombs were dropped, and I automatically hunched my shoulders as I heard them whistling down.

It had become comparatively quiet as I got into my overcoat. Putting out the lights, I opened the flat door. My pipe I kept conspicuously alight, the idea being to allay suspicion.

Down the stairs, past the stirrup pump and the subdued lights. There was a queer, painful thrill in my heart that was not unpleasant.

CHAPTER II

THERE WERE two doors to the building, the first acting as a light trap when the outer was opened. I went through the first and stood in the dark for a moment. Strangely enough, I did not feel worried, only curious; it would be interesting to see what the police intended to do. From the High Street, sounding like a call to freedom, came a swirl of muffled traffic.

With a wry smile I opened the door and went down the steps. There was no sign of anyone. Then the faintest of faint noises from the area; someone was down there—waiting.

It was a beautiful night; cold, crisp and clear. There was a quarter moon, and its hard, metallic light lit the upper part of the houses. The rest was painted with shadows, the lovely deep purple that moon and the night can create. The white-shuttered windows of the buildings gleamed ghost-like.

No one else was in the street; at least, they were not to be seen. A hundred yards away the park railings were clearly visible. Sometimes a wraith-like omnibus swept them momentarily from view.

I walked slowly towards those railings. I had no idea if any move had been made by the waiting man. Perhaps they had given some signal. Possibly there were other watchers ahead of me.

I crossed the main road. Along the railings I went, looking at the trees in the park, whose branches wealed a lace-like pattern against the white night. A gate was open, and above it an illuminated S with an arrow pointing to the shelters.

The sky was a carpet of stars.

Did I say it was a lovely night? It was a lousy one. The moon had come up and driven off my friend the darkness.

It had seemed easy in the flat. All I had to do was to melt away in the night. But who the devil could melt in this light?

There were no people about. The sparse traffic rushed by in a hurry to get home—dimly-lit omnibuses looking like torches whose batteries have run down, taxis like giant blackbeetles; and above, that confounded moon shone with approving brightness on the scene.

I reached the bus stop opposite Gloucester Road, and stamped about to keep warm. A hundred yards away a car was parked by the pavement; obviously a police car. Then a man sauntered across the road, and stopping at the bus stop, casually lit a cigarette. He appeared engrossed in watching the sky—too engrossed. He was a detective all right.

Along came a No. 9 bus. I went on top. The cigarette smoker, throwing away his cigarette, went inside.

It was dark up there, for the black-hooded lights gave but a faint glow. Sitting in the back seat was a soldier with his arm round a girl. They had no time for anything but each other. In the front was a man who was singing. No one else.

I sat down, and then took a look round to see if the police-car was following. There was mesh-work on the glass and some glazed paint to stop splintering, if we met up with a bomb. It looked nice and safe, but you could not see a thing through it.

We went at a cracking pace along moon-flooded Kensington Gore. As far as I was concerned, we went a damn sight too fast. Somehow I had to beat those policemen before we reached Piccadilly. This left me just about ten minutes in which to work a miracle.

I put it in the form of a problem. The police would let anyone off the bus, provided that person was not Michael Stephen. So, to get off, all that was necessary was a change of identity. The question was how could that be worked.

Something had to be done. So I went up to the one person who might help—the man singing in the front seat. To be accurate, he had stopped singing. He was leaning back languidly, and cast bleary eyes at me as I sat down. He appeared delighted to find someone with whom to talk. I soon learnt a great deal about him. His wife and children had been evacuated, and he had been given a day off to visit them. Jumping lorries to save the fare back, he had landed up at Barnes. There had, clearly, been no lack of liquid refreshment on the way.

Medium-sized, about fifty, with a walrus moustache and a worried brow, he had a habit of punctuating his remarks with a prod of his finger; he spoke confidentially and close to me, and all he said was accompanied by the odour of beer. The whispered proximity of his conversation gave one the impression that he was about to impart some significant secret. At his feet was a canvas hold-all, and in his left hand he clutched something wrapped in newspaper. It smelt strongly of fish. This gift from his wife presented a problem.

"Two 'addocks," he muttered morosely. "She ses, you take 'em an' eat properly. But I asks yer, 'ow am I going to cook 'em? Wot I 'ave ter do ter-night is to get someone to tell me 'ow."

I bore the proximity of his breath with fortitude, because an idea was emerging.

But time was pressing. Already the bus was moving to a stop near the Hyde Park Hotel. With covetous eyes I regarded my companion's battered bowler and yellow mackintosh.

"Look here," I said. "What do you want for your hat and coat?"

"'Ow do you mean?"

"I want to buy them."

"Woffer?"

I thought quickly.

"For a bet. It's worth ten pounds to me if I can walk home to-night in someone else's coat and hat."

He eyed me suspiciously.

"'Ow much?"

"I'll give you three pounds."

The possibility of a deal sobered him somewhat. But he was uncertain and distrustful. I took out the money and gave it to him.

"Mind yer—it's for keeps. You can't 'ave it back!" He sat there looking first at the money and then at me. Obviously he thought there was a catch somewhere.

"Come on," I said, impatiently.

He suddenly gave me a cold look.

"Naw, your 'aving a game with me. This money's no good!"

"Of course it's good. Look at it."

I swore under my breath. I was so near to getting what I wanted; and here was this fool, befuddled by drink, holding me up.

"What makes you think it's no good?" I asked.

"You ain't got no bet. I wasn't born yesterday, yer know."

This was maddening, until I saw how the situation could be turned to my advantage.

"I'll tell you what I'll do," I said. "We'll get off the bus together and have a drink. They'll change that money in a pub."

His face lit up.

"That's different. But you 'ave to be careful, see wot I mean! No offence, mate?"

He took off his hat and raincoat. I put them on, stuffing my own under the seat. This last act drew a protest from my companion; but I got him moving at last, by going back to the drink question. He picked up his canvas hold-all and I, for my own purpose, offered to carry it. As the bus slowed up for a stop he began to descend the steps. I followed, prepared to play my part for all I was worth. There was a danger that the detective had asked the conductor how many people were on top. If he had done this, then there was no hope. But I was gambling on the fact that he would not think it necessary.

Turning up the collar of the yellow mackintosh and tilting the angle of the bowler, I went cluttering down the steps.

"Wot a life, eh!" sang out my friend, drunkenly and joyously. "Bombs and everything."

"Never you mind that, chum," I shouted thickly. "We'll have a drink before they get us."

The conductor was standing on the platform.

"Steady, mate," he said to my lurching companion.

The detective was sitting just inside, watching us. So I held up the hold-all to cover my face. My companion stopped to argue the point with the conductor; but I wanted him off, because at any moment a remark might be made about the raincoat changing hands. I gave him a push which sent him stumbling on to the pavement.

The detective half rose in his seat, and my heart raced. Then he sank back. Getting off, I linked arms with my new friend, and we began to move with uncertain steps along the pavement. We were at Hyde Park Corner.

Soon our omnibus started up and passed us. Then, in a few seconds, came the police car. They went on into the silver night towards Piccadilly. I was safe—for the moment.

The columns at the entrance to the Park gleamed in the moonlight; two policemen, steel-helmeted, with service gas masks strapped on their backs, watched us with a detached air. My companion was waving the packet of fish, while he performed an intricate song and dance. The sooner we got to the public-house the better. I dare not leave him, because, if I did so, he would most certainly create a scene. It would be just my luck if the police got me through arresting him.

"Steady," I said, "or the coppers will nab us."

"Coppers! Never mind the . . . coppers! Wot about our drink?"

But it quietened him down a bit. I turned back towards Knightsbridge, arguing that the police would expect me to go the other way.

Walking along the stretch between Hyde Park Corner and the Albert Gate was something of a trial. We went past a cab shelter, and my companion nearly fell into a horse drinking-trough. As we reached the closed and shuttered shops, he suddenly gave tongue. To a passer-by he shouted: "'Ere, mate, 'ow do you cook an 'addock?"

The stranger went on, his face averted. Luckily there were few people about.

The gun-fire had died down to an occasional burst. But in the direction of the docks a red glow in the sky showed that a fire had been started. We plunged into Lowndes Square. In the roadway my foot knocked against something that tinkled like glass. It was a piece of shrapnel about half the size of my hand.

Finally we got to a mews and a public-house. Pushing aside the black-out curtain, we found ourselves in a cosy warm fug.

My companion went for the bar like a homing pigeon. Cocking an eye at me, he muttered man's kindliest question: "Wot's yours?"

He paid with one of my pound notes, and gave me a knowing smile as he got his change. His drink couldn't have gone quicker if it had been poured into the desert sands.

Only a few people were present. Two of the men were in the blue overalls of the A.F.S., and there was a girl in the same fire-fighting service.

I got my companion to sit down while I ordered another round. Putting a hand into the pocket of the raincoat I made a discovery. There were some papers, including my friend's identity card and ration book. After a bit of quick thinking, the identity card went into my own pocket.

His suspicions about the money dissolved, my friend became quite affable. He told me his name was Wicket, and of his troubles now that his wife was evacuated. I looked at him with interest, here was a member of a new breed—the married bachelor.

A fat man came through the black-out curtains into the pub, sniffed the fish, and said, "Where are we—Billingsgate?"

Wicket said: "'Ow do you cook an' 'addock?"

"Sit on it," said the newcomer.

My companion gave him a look of drunken dignity, and, going to the bar, repeated his question.

The publican, however, turned away to switch on the wireless. It was just on nine o'clock. The preceding part of the programme had finished; but to signal the station came the irritating three notes B.B.C. struck on a piano. It sounded like a lazy piano tuner at work. Then the chimes of Big Ben, and the announcer's voice: "This is the B.B.C. Home Service; here is the news and this is Frank Phillips reading it."

There was news of our push in Libya, and two enemy aircraft had been shot down off the South Coast.

Everyone listened in silence. Then the announcer said, "That is the end of the news, and before the postscript here is a police message."

Conversation started again. Wicket, banging on the bar with his fish, demanded a cooking lesson.

I, however, listened intently to the loudspeaker; and for a good reason. *The subject of the police message was myself.*

"The police are anxious to find a man called Michael Stephen, alias Carr," said the voice. "He has been seen to-night in the West End of London. He was wearing a dark blue suit, and a red tie with polka dots, and possibly a raincoat." Here my description followed. "Should you have any information concerning this man, or any suspicion that you have seen him, inform your local police station, or telephone Scotland Yard, Whitehall 1212. If you meet anyone answering this description, get the help of the police, or a member of the armed forces or A.R.P. workers, as he should be detained until his identity can be checked. Do not attempt to tackle him yourself. I will repeat this."

That message was the surprise of my life. The police had been quick; and it proved that the show was bigger than I had thought, or the broadcast would never have been made.

I shrunk into the raincoat, feeling lost. Surely everything was over? The bar was well lit. No one could mistake me. My only hope was the English mind, which refuses to dramatize events.

Wicket, unknowingly, was helping me. Banging the fish on the bar, he was making such a scene that everyone's attention was on him. The publican told him to be quiet.

With great dignity Wicket replied: "I only want ter know 'ow ter cook an' 'addock!"

"Well, don't make such a barney about it—or it's outside for you!"

Whereupon my companion turned to address the room. He looked sadder than ever. The injustice of his treatment was rankling.

"If a man's not entitled to ask a question, wot are we fighting this bloody war for? I ask civil like; I expect a civil answer."

Wicket had had enough.

The others regarded him with shy, sly grins. The wireless announcer repeated the police message practically unheeded.

Then a small man at the end of the bar said: "That's a funny police message. Who do you think this bloke is?"

"I wasn't listening properly," said the fat man.

I tried to join in the conversation, in an effort to appear at ease. But at that moment I could not trust my voice. Dully, like someone in a dream, I listened while they discussed me.

"I'll tell you what I think. The police might want him because he's a Fifth Columnist who's been signalling. That goes on, you know."

The fat man nodded.

"Maybe. But it just shows yer that people don't listen. Now I didn't get 'is description. Something about a raincoat—"

It was the turn of the small man to nod.

"Dark feller in a blue suit," he said.

The publican put in a word.

"Red tie—hadn't he got!"

I felt a line of perspiration on my brow, and my mouth—despite the beer—felt dry. The collar of the raincoat was turned up; this covered the tie. But the description had been very clear. If they fitted together a few more fragments, they must arrive at a complete picture of myself.

Again Wicket came to my rescue.

He asked the A.F.S. girl to have a drink, and turned to be served. The publican shook his head.

"You've had enough."

"Enough!" This baffled Wicket for a moment. Then he said, thickly, "Are they rationing beer as well?"

"If they are," said the fat man, "you've 'ad your little lot for the war, to-night."

An argument appeared to be developing. I gave a casual "good-night" and made for the door. But my departure caused Wicket to break off the discussion. The mention of rationing had started a train of thought.

"'Ere, where are you going?" he shouted. "You've got me ration cards in me coat."

I stopped.

"'Ere, common, give us 'em!" Wicket moved unsteadily towards me. To the room at large he said, "Do you know something? Three pun' this bloke gives me for me 'at and coat. I asks yer, three oncers!"

This surely must arouse their suspicion? If Wicket went on it would all come out. The deal on the bus, the stuffing of my hat and coat under the seat. Once they investigated me they would see the red tie. Even now, it seemed, the fat man was regarding me with a suspicious look in his eyes.

There was a double problem. Not only had I got to get out myself, but I must take Wicket with me. He could not be left to amplify his story.

"Your trouble is that you always get drunk!" I shouted thickly. "And now you're calling me a thief! Come on!"

I struck out and caught him a glancing blow. He went back, surprised rather than hurt. The fat man jumped between us, shouting, "'Ere! 'Ere!" The publican came round his bar in a flash. Grasping hold of both of us, he hustled us to the door.

"No fighting here!" he stormed. "Outside! Both of you!"

We, were pushed out into the cold moonlight. I, thankfully; Wicket, indignantly. In a few seconds a hold-all and a packet of fish followed us into the mews.

I still had to get Wicket out of the neighbourhood— for my own safety. He was cursing freely; fortunately his invective was directed against the publican.

Giving him back his hat and coat, which had become a danger to me, I steered him into a taxi. Before I slammed the door on him, Wicket wanted to know if the driver could cook a haddock.

The ack-ack guns had started again. So I decided to try one of London's underground dormitories. Knightsbridge Station was the nearest, and was sufficiently close to my point of escape to make it improbable that the police would search there. Someone sheltering in a doorway coughed, and the sound made me start. I had become a hunted man looking over his shoulder.

I took a three-halfpenny ticket and went down the escalator. At the bottom an A.R.P. warden was talking to a policeman. Dry-mouthed, I passed them.

The platform presented a strange sight.

The tier-bunks were full; and on the ground were rows of recumbent people. Men, women and children, all packed together like sardines. Most of them lay on rugs or coats, with just enough room to stretch full length.

Some of the people were already asleep. One man lay with his mouth wide open; he slept soundly, despite the noise of a train that had just drawn into the station. Others were sitting up, talking. A few of the women were knitting, and four men played cards. They did not look a depressed lot. There was a canteen affair, and a first-aid post complete with a uniformed nurse.

I suppose these people worked, ate, and then came straight to this slightly fetid atmosphere. That was their whole existence. In many cases their small bundles represented their sole worldly possessions.

The sooner I was lost in this sea of humanity the better. Near one end were two middle-aged women. They seemed friendly; and, what was more to the point, there was an empty space beside them.

"Any chance of sleeping here?" I asked.

One of them, dressed in a brown coat, looked up sympathetically.

"You can 'ave my 'usband's place; 'e's over Neasden way to-night, sleeping at 'is sister's place."

Originally, they explained to me, they had slept in bunks, but had given them up in preference for the ground, as this was less draughty. The thin one pointed at a man who slept with his head inside an upturned suitcase.

"You get a bit of a blow down 'ere sometimes, an' that keeps the light and draught off your face. Once the last train's gone, you get a nice night's sleep, between about one and six."

They asked me if it was "quiet up top," explaining that we were eighty feet down and couldn't hear much of the blitz. They debated the merits of various underground stations. They had a bad opinion of Tottenham Court Road Station. It was not, they considered, one of London's better run shelters. For that matter, they took a poor view of most West End stations; it appeared that these attracted the riff-raff. Hampstead, they had been told, was very deep, and there was a nodding of heads over this virtue; against this, so their information had it, the air was not so good. But then you could not expect everything.

Then the thin one looked along the platform of Knightsbridge Station, with a complacent air:

"But 'ere," she said, "you get a real nice lot of people. You don't 'ave to worry."

Soon I settled down; not to sleep, but to think. The police would be active, and sooner or later they must find me. My only hope of prolonging the hunt would be to alter my appearance.

But the real problem was to find Carr. Freedom was useless unless it led to him. But where could I look for him? I began sorting out my information.

What did I know? Well, there was the pub in Kensington High Street. But the man in the raincoat had seen me. Ten to one he knew I had been arrested. If he knew, Carr knew. Right, that put the pub off my double's visiting list.

What else did I know?

Carr looked like me. That was something. . . . Then a disturbing thought. If Carr knew of my arrest he would go to ground. He would not be found sauntering round the streets. I concentrated like mad. My mind went over everything; my arrest, the trip to Scotland Yard, the questioning.

Then I got it. Or, rather, I got something.

The grey-haired man at Scotland Yard had said, "I see you no longer smoke your Pagani black cigars."

So I did know one thing about Carr. He smoked Pagani cigars!

It was little enough, God knows. But it gave me hope. On the morrow I would change my appearance; my hunt would begin for a man who smoked Pagani's black cigars.

My "bed" was hard and uncomfortable, but soon I slept. In my dreams I followed a man down a long dark tunnel. Only his back was to be seen, but in his hand he carried an enormous black cigar. Try as I might, it was impossible to overtake him.

The floor was slippery; there were bomb craters into which I nearly fell. Suddenly my quarry turned. I gave a gasp. On his face was a mask, a grotesque caricature of myself. This split into a grin, and he said, "I'm you!"

Then the police came after me, chasing me into the depths of the earth. My feet were like lead; I could scarcely move. The wall behind which I sought to hide dissolved into nothing.

There was no escape. I groaned as they took me.

CHAPTER III

I woke round about six, stiff and cramped. Trains were running again, and sleepy people were performing their perfunctory toilet. Slowly this strange section of humanity broke up and went to work. I said good-bye to my hostesses and took a train to Piccadilly Circus.

At the Coventry Street Corner House I borrowed a razor from the cloakroom attendant, a common enough request in these days. Then I bought a newspaper, and buried myself behind this in the restaurant.

I looked for some reference to myself, but there was nothing. Not even a mention of the police wireless message. This comforted me. Perhaps I had been too gloomy. After all, the police were busy. I had only to use a little sense to be all right. I felt confident as I paid my bill and went out. Too confident, as it happened.

The problem of disguise had been occupying my mind, and I decided that a change of clothes would help. My present outfit was on the formal side, so I was going for the opposite effect. Grey flannel trousers, sports coat, an arty tie and a pork-pie hat; and horn-rimmed spectacles.

The shops were not yet open, so I strolled along Shaftesbury Avenue. Then, like a damn fool, I pulled out my pipe. At the corner of a street I struck a match.

I deserved what happened. I should have realized that pipe smoking would be one of my habits known to the authorities.

A policeman, standing on the corner, started forward.

"Hey, I want you," he said.

If he had seized me without talking, it would have been all over. There was a good many people about. I would not have had a chance. As it was, he made the mistake of opening his mouth. It gave me time to realize my danger. I turned to him as if I were going to stop, and replied with an innocent, "Me?" But I was on my toes, ready for a dash.

He came towards me, pointing a finger.

"You're Michael Stephen, aren't you?"

In an instant I was off up the side street, running like mad. Behind me the policeman shouted, "Hey, come back! . . . Stop that man! Stop him!"

One or two people turned, gaping at me. It all happened so quickly that I was past them before they grasped the situation. A man made a half-hearted attempt to grab me, but a swerve took me away from him.

The gap between the policeman and myself was widening. I have always been a good runner, and he was handicapped by his steel helmet, coat and gas-mask. He did not blow a whistle. Presumably it was against regulations.

Behind me came a patter of feet and some shouting. The hunt was growing. There were people waiting at the top of the street, and once they realized what it was all about, they would stop me. So I shot into an alley-way. It was short and led into a busy thoroughfare.

A man lounged in a doorway.

"Get inside," I shouted, "time-bomb!"

I half pushed him into the house, and followed myself. The door shut as the pursuit turned the corner.

"What's that?" asked the man.

"We're working on a time-bomb, but it's a new type. It's going off. So we had to get out quick."

The story was thin, but he seemed to believe it. In the hall-way was a cloakroom and a reception desk. It was some sort of a day club. My host was probably the porter or caretaker.

"Wait here," he said, "I'll get the keys of the cellar."

He went through a doorway, and I changed my plan. There were a few coats and hats hanging up. Possibly their owners slept in the building. Anyway, I helped myself. There was no time to waste. The porter would soon be coining back, so I had to risk the outside being safe.

A few seconds later I was walking down the alley-way, guilty of the theft of a hat and overcoat.

I turned back towards Shaftesbury Avenue. People were still standing about, talking; they took no notice of me, which was understandable. It could not occur to them that I was the hatless and coatless individual who had so recently sprinted towards them.

I jumped on a No. 22 omnibus. Luck had been with me, but it had been a bit of a shock. If a policeman on a beat carried my description in his head, I would have to look out. The sooner my appearance was altered the better.

I got off in Holborn. There was a Woolworths, and here I bought a pair of horn-rimmed spectacles. At

Gamages I got an overcoat, a pork-pie hat, and the rest of my outfit.

I finished by getting a suitcase and shaving materials. The tobacco department told me that the only place in London for Pagani's cigars was at Kalpini's, of Bond Street.

I changed in a public lavatory, and shoved my old stuff into the suitcase. It is wonderful what a change different type of clothes and a pair of glasses can make. The suitcase I left at King's Cross Station cloakroom.

There remained one thing to do before the hunt for Carr began, and at a post office I sent a letter-card to Inspector Cartwright, of Scotland Yard, the gist of my message being that I was not the man they wanted; and, though they might not believe this, they should look for the real Carr, as well as for myself.

Then by underground to Bond Street Station. My destination was Kalpini's tobacco shop, and those Pagani's cigars.

As my eyes searched for Kalpini's shop, a curious feeling of anticipation stirred inside me. London's smart shopping centre had not escaped the War. Here and there wooden boards covered the windows that had once displayed expensive goods. But beautifully dressed women still strolled up and down, looking into the reduced window space of Fenwick's, Asprey's, and other shops.

Kalpini's was at the Piccadilly end of the street. It dealt in expensive cigarettes and cigars. There was nothing remarkable about it, except that the plate-glass was intact; this allowed one a full view of its interior.

I hurried past. I do not quite know why; unless it was an instinct that told me not to hang about. No shadow of a plan had as yet suggested itself to me.

I went to the end of Bond Street, and then walked slowly back on the other side. I came abreast of Kalpini's once more and went on past it. By the side of an art shop was a doorway, and acting on impulse, I went through it.

I found myself in a dark panelled hall-way. At the bottom of the stairs was a board indicating the names of the tenants.

I stood there, turning things over in my mind. It was obvious that Kalpini could only be of help if Carr went there for his cigars. He might come in a week, he might come in a month; he might never come at all.

I had come into the building to think, but now realized that it had other possibilities. Suppose there was somewhere here in which to keep observation?

I went up the thickly carpeted stairs.

Outside the door on the first floor was a metal disc. This bore the name of Mrs. Baggot. But what interested me was the letter-box; because, sticking through the flap of this was a newspaper. I pushed this newspaper through, and as I held up the flap of the letter-box I could see inside; on the floor were other newspapers and several letters. Mrs. Baggot was not in residence.

Now, if it were possible to get into the flat, it might be just what I wanted. The door, of course, was locked. But I felt under the carpet, and there was the key; so

I unlocked the door and went, somewhat cautiously, into the flat.

The door led straight into a large room overlooking the street. At the back was another room, a bedroom, kitchen and bathroom. The place was pleasantly furnished.

Kalpini's, on the other side, was a few doors down the street. It was possible to see not only the shop itself, but the partitioned section behind; and seated in the back part was my friend the dark-jowled detective.

The presence of the police might make it risky, but it confirmed my hunch. There *was* a chance of Carr coming; at any rate, the police must think so. They were waiting, despite the grey-haired man's indirect warning to myself.

But there might be snags. Supposing Mrs. Baggot returned? I took a look round. Newspapers pushed through the letter-box covered four days. That seemed to settle the date she had left. But the flat was spotless. It looked as though a cleaner came in daily. If I was caught I would have to say that Mrs. Baggot had lent me the flat.

The other point was the situation across the street. If the real Carr turned up, then all would be well. I take it that he would be arrested on the spot. I could then reveal myself, and the show would be over.

I went out to do some shopping, and set off up Bond Street at a smart pace. The street had become a trap, so there was none of my earlier, carefree sauntering. At Selfridges I bought a pair of binoculars, and some food.

From the flat window I focussed the binoculars on to Kalpini's. The detail of everything was remarkably clear. I could even read the lettering on some of the cigarette boxes. Then I paused and gazed with fixed intensity on some boxes at the end of a shelf. There were green labels stuck on them, and in white lettering the name *Pagani's Cigars.*

This was the bait. All we wanted now was our fish.

At first I watched, breathlessly, everyone who entered the shop. But soon my enthusiasm waned. I began to sympathize with the waiting detective. I, too, was bored. Optimism ebbed a trifle. It was impossible to ignore the fact that Carr might not come.

My attention strayed to the street.

I noticed that people moved more quickly, with greater purpose, for over all of them hung the threat of that modern curfew—the black-out.

The next morning I was back at the window, watching. It was a boring business; only the importance of the issue made it worth while.

Time went damnably slowly. I began to play a game, betting myself that a woman in trousers would pass with the next five. Then I fiddled with the gadgets round the flat. One of these was an automatic cigarette-lighter made in the form of a revolver.

A newspaper had been pushed through the letter-box, and later, letters were delivered. But it began to look as though this was not the cleaner's day.

A lethargic coma began stealing over me. My watch told me it was three twenty-two. I yawned.

The next moment I was wide awake. A key was turning in the lock. Someone was coming into the flat.

CHAPTER IV

IT WAS Mrs. Baggot. At least, I guessed it was.

My hostess was fat, middle-aged. She made one think of cream buns and tea, of bridge and gossip. Her clothes would have been admirable on someone fifteen years younger.

When she saw me she gave an "Oh" of surprise. I think her first impression was that she had entered the wrong flat. She did not look alarmed. In fact, unless I was mistaken, she seemed rather pleased. I, for my part, felt strangely at ease.

"Mrs. Baggot?" I managed, lightly. "My name is Scott."

She seemed to find nothing strange in the fact that an unknown man was in her flat. Putting down her suitcase, she began peeling off her gloves. Then, without any warning, conversation rattled from her lips.

"Scott?" she repeated. "My dear boy, not the Scotts from Dorking. But I've known them for years. My dearest friends. It's extraordinary, because I met someone the other day who knew someone I knew when I was a girl. That's forty years ago; well, thirty. I can remember them as well as I can you. Or someone I know, rather."

I smiled.

"I'm afraid I've no relations at Dorking."

"Haven't you! It's just as well. I don't like them. . . . But who let you in here? I suppose Mrs. Wade did. I wonder, did she ring up those people for me! Servants never remember. It's just what I said to

Mrs. Chase; I don't know whether you know her! Her husband's a colonel. And her daughter went to Cheltenham—or Roedean. The daughter's very plain—but charming. I told Mrs. Chase not to worry about her. Someone will marry her."

I dragged her back to present realities.

"I let myself in."

"You naughty man! Did you want to see me?"

"Not exactly, you see I'm really a trespasser. As a matter of fact, I've been here since yesterday."

She gave me a look. You could see the struggle in her mind. The romancer *versus* the outraged householder.

"But why have you come here!"

By this time I had a story calculated to suit Mrs. Baggot. I lifted up the binoculars.

"I came here to watch. It probably seems completely crazy to you. But you see—" here some emotion entered my voice, "—I'm hopelessly in love with someone. Unfortunately, she's married. She and her husband live across the road here. This is the only way I can get a sight of her."

I paused—then, with feeling: "I hope you can sympathize and not think too badly of me!"

I need not have worried. She was the type that sympathized with young men, all right. Of course, the story sounded thin; and for a moment my hostess hesitated. But it was clear that she would not permit disbelief in anything savouring of intrigue.

"But how romantic!" she exclaimed, and insisted on being shown the window of the "loved one."

"Then you don't mind?" I asked.

"Mind! Of course, I don't mind. You must come here as often as you like."

I took her hand. It seemed the right thing to do. She did not withdraw. Instead, she gave me a warm pressure of understanding.

"It's very nice of you to trust me," I said.

Mrs. Baggot drew herself up.

"Of course, I trust you. I can read people. My dear boy, I have a friend at Scotland Yard. *I know*!"

Mrs. Baggot insisted on my sleeping at the flat. She, herself, stayed with a friend. Every day she came round full of advice and questions. She wallowed in the intrigue. I have never seen anyone enjoy themselves so much.

Soon I had to invent items. The "wife's" name was Mercia and her "husband" was Bruce. Naturally, I could not disclose their surname. Mrs. Baggot, though she was disappointed, nodded her head in understanding. But how she thrilled when I described "Bruce's" torture of his wife. Not physically, of course. He was far too clever for that. But mentally. He was cruel to the point of genius. His hold on her was the child, aged two. She could not leave him, for that would mean losing her little daughter.

Discreetly, but persistently, my hostess edged round the question of paternity. Was I fond of the child? Did the husband love it? With a wistful look I left this part undisclosed. Mrs. Baggot drew her own conclusions.

The situation had turned to my advantage. I spent the day at my post, watching, with, at times, large doses of Mrs. Baggot's Jumping Jack conversation.

My reluctance to go out, I explained, being due to the danger of meeting "Bruce."

To the cleaner, Mrs. Wade, I was introduced as "Cousin Anthony." Mrs. Baggot, with a girlish simper, had suggested this. "You know how people talk!"

Mrs. Baggot was a great letter writer. She penned words to her own Member of Parliament, and to other people's. She wrote to Mr. Eden at the Foreign Office, telling him how to win the war. On receiving no reply, she delivered a snub both cutting and final. She discontinued the correspondence. Her letters now went direct to Mr. Churchill.

There was a great deal of Old England in her. The possibility of defeat did not exist. Her statements were often outrages; she was rather stupid, irritatingly complacent and invariably muddled. But she possessed something that England possesses—character.

I grew fond of her.

There had been a series of fire-bombs on London. But Mrs. Baggot was ready. She had her statistics.

"People wouldn't worry," she said, "if they realized how little there is of London. I mean, houses compared to open spaces. I have a friend at Westminster Town Hall, and *I know*! In Greater London only fifteen per cent is property. And we have millions of agents in Germany. Well, anyway, a lot. And do you know the chances of being hit by a bomb? It's only one per cent of something per cent! And Churchill says it will take a hundred years, or some such time, to demolish London. On an average, and on that basis, we'll all live till the year 2141—I think it was. That's two hundred years. Well, that is, we would, of course, if we could live that long. So Hitler can't possibly kill me. Because if I'm not an average human being, I should like to know who is!"

Her flow of words could always be checked by the mention of "Mercia." Under pressure of questioning, that phantom was rapidly taking shape in my mind.

She was dark and slim and incredibly sweet. I felt like the creator of Pygmalion. Finally, I became quite fond of this imaginary creature. Mrs. Baggot, of course, was enchanted. She thought this idealistic love wonderful. My patient watch, my hopeless love. For it was hopeless. I never saw "Mercia." (Incidentally, I saw no signs of my more tangible quarry—Carr.)

Mrs. Baggot was full of schemes to effect a meeting. It was with difficulty that I persuaded her against visiting "Mercia." Almost her entire interest was now centred on this "love triangle."

I could not but think that luck had come my way. Not many people would have believed my story. I settled down to a dull but safe existence. There were now three detectives waiting at Kalpini's. They took it in turns to keep watch.

Five days passed before the blow fell.

It happened one misty morning. Mrs. Baggot had not yet arrived. Suddenly I felt cramped and damnably bored. Whatever it cost, I was going out to stretch my legs.

The weather was favourable, visibility being poor, and the sleet that was falling would make it natural for a man to huddle down in his coat. Coming out I went to a public- house, feeling rather like a truant schoolboy.

I had a couple of drinks, and then got chatting to a young Canadian soldier. We got on to Roosevelt. I have a big opinion of that fellow. It seems to me that when posterity estimates this period of history, Roosevelt may well be called America's greatest Statesman. He is one of the few men alive capable of understanding man, in the same way as Hitler does. The difference between the two seems to be that Hitler manages humanity by getting at their baser qualities; and it is a regrettable fact that this method should be so successful. The American, however, gets at them by appealing to their finer instincts. This way may be slower, but it is apt to last. We discussed the chances of America coming into the War (this was, of course, before Japan launched her treacherous attack in December, 1941).

I dare not stay long away from my post, and the last Scotch went down quickly. I walked up Bond Street in a nonchalant manner, letting myself into the flat with a key given me by Mrs. Baggot.

My hostess was sitting at a table. I knew at once that something had happened, for she was in a state of suppressed excitement. She gave me a look, and then lowered her face with a smile. It looked as though she had some surprise up her sleeve for me. She had!

"You are a lucky boy!" she said; simpering.

She gave a girlish giggle. Then glanced at the door leading to the other part of the flat. I also looked in that direction. It was clear that there lay the surprise.

I smiled.

"Have you got something for me?"

"Something! . . . *Someone!*"

"Someone!" My heart nearly missed a beat. I was too astonished to speak.

"Who?" I finally croaked.

"You'll never guess. They're in there."

Mrs. Baggot pointed at the door; I seemed to stop thinking. Anyone who knew me could only be a danger. It was a trap—the police! But the Scotch, which had quickened my wits, now appeared to stupefy me. I should have run. Instead, I stood and gaped.

"Aren't you going to see who it is?"

I had a feeling that my face was very white.

"You must tell me who it is," I gasped.

"You must see for yourself!"

"Do I know them?"

"Oh, yes."

"No—look here! You must tell me. It's important!"

Mrs. Baggot could contain herself no longer. Her body was quivering with a delicious thrill. She went up to the connecting door and flung it open.

"It's Mercia!" she cried.

A dark, slim girl came into the room. I had never seen her before in my life.

CHAPTER V

WE STARED at each other, an unfathomable look in her dark eyes; surprise, bewilderment—presumably—in mine. I could have done several things. I should have said, "This isn't Mercia!" —or else I should have run away.

I said nothing.

Mrs. Baggot stood by the doorway, thrilled. She must have felt like an impresario who has staged her big scene. As neither of us spoke, she whispered, "Go on!"

Something had to be done.

"Hullo, darling!" I said, in a voice that sounded like nothing on earth.

"Hullo, Tony," said "Mercia."

Her voice was soft; at the moment rather expressionless. It conveyed nothing of which she might be thinking. I had no idea why she pretended to know me. Or what she expected of me.

Mrs. Baggot saved me. I can only conclude that she mistook our silence for lovers' rapture. She began to speak, crackling off like machine-gun fire.

"Mr. Scott! No—I'm going to call you Tony, too. I insist. Isn't it wonderful! I found Mercia and arranged it all. That is, actually she found me; and she arranged it. But she said, 'You must keep it a surprise.' She came up to me as I was coming in here. 'Are you Mrs. Baggot?' she asked. So, of course, I said 'Yes,' because I am. And then I asked her how she knew me. And she just said, 'I'm Mercia! I live across

the street!' I wouldn't believe it. I couldn't believe it!
Though, of course, I did. I've never been so surprised
in my life. And thrilled—oh, my dear, I was thrilled!
I thought of all your patient waiting—and here was
your reward. But it's quite all right."

Here Mrs. Baggot discreetly lowered her voice.

"Her husband—Bruce, you know—is away. So you
needn't worry. Well, of course, I suggested lunch. I
mean, I had to. Mrs. Wade's got some champagne; so
it's going to be a real celebration. . . . Now I'm going
to leave you, because I know you have a lot to say to
each other. Well, naturally!"

She embraced us both with a look.

"Oh, my dears!" she sighed ecstatically.

The next moment the connecting door opened and
closed. Mrs. Baggot was exercising tact, delicacy and
understanding. She had gone.

I looked at "Mercia." No mistaking the unfriendly
look in her eyes now. The first shock over, my brain
was clearing and I felt damnably curious about this
girl. Obviously she had not come from the police. If
they knew I was here—it would have meant strong
arm tactics.

But she knew about Mercia. She knew Mrs. Baggot's name. How? I tried to read something from her
face. But could only reflect that she was an attractive
creature. Dark eyes, an oval face and a silky complexion that, I suppose, one should describe as olive. All
this in a flash, because at once she said:

"Perhaps you'll tell me what you're doing here?"

The situation was so unexpected, so fantastic, I
could not resist a flippancy:

"To meet you, Mercia!"

"You pretended to know me. So there isn't a Mercia, is there?"

"Before I answer that, you've got to tell me who you are!" I said.

Attack was my only form of defence. Her position could not be too happy. After all, she was an interloper. I went on:

"My dear girl, you come bursting in here on a false name. You don't know Mrs. Baggot and you don't know me. But you've got the nerve to cross-question me. It's a bit too much. Suppose I go to Mrs. Baggot about you! You're not going to like that!"

Mercia sunk me with one sentence. Confound it. She seemed damned sure of her ground.

"Suppose we both go to Mrs. Baggot!"

I tried a feeble last shot.

"I wouldn't bluff, if I were you. The next step will be the police."

She smiled, but the glint did not leave her eyes.

"We'll go there first, if you like."

That seemed to be that. So, I altered my tactics.

"How did you hear about Mercia?" I asked. "I only pretended to know you to save you embarrassment."

"You got in here by lying," she said, ignoring my question.

"So did you!" I retorted.

"I warn you, I really am going to the police!" Her face was set and grim as she said this.

I shrugged my shoulders.

"Why? I'm a friend of Mrs. Baggot's."

"I'm waiting," she said.

"No, no. You've got to tell me something about yourself. After all, I've a right to that. I do at least know Mrs. Baggot; but you're a stranger to us both. You might be anybody. You must prove your *bona fides* to me. Suppose you were a dishonest person!"

"That's funny, coming from you."

"I admire your nerve, but not your manners."

"Mercia" hesitated, then:

"All right. But I warn you I'm not as credulous as Mrs. Baggot."

She looked me full in the face when she spoke. It seemed to be a habit. Her eyes were frank—and very lovely.

"Mrs. Baggot is a friend of my aunt," she said, "and she told my aunt about finding you here and of your story of a love affair with Mercia. It sounded ridiculous."

"Not to those with a sense of romance."

"Mrs. Baggot doesn't know me, so I came along to find out just why you are here."

I tried to look incredulous.

"Don't you believe me?"

"No."

This was a tricky turn to the business. It might mean all sorts of trouble. For this girl intended to be satisfied. Curiously enough, my main feeling was one of buoyancy and relief. That sounds ridiculous, but there it was. I had been buried, and here was something turning up. The girl looked frightfully intent and a little strung up—as she had a right to be. After all, she could have had no idea of the person she was going to face when she took on the job.

"Why didn't you go to the police in the first place?" I asked, with genuine curiosity.

"There's plenty of time for that!" She glanced out of the window. "There's one out there in the street now."

Something would have to be done. There was, as she had pointed out, a policeman in the street; and across the road were detectives waiting for me. Any sort of a show-down would be fatal. I would have to bluff. Lie like hell and get out. This girl was no fool.

I took a step towards her, with, I hope, a look of engaging frankness on my face.

"Look here, you're quite right, Miss—er—" I hesitated, but she did not supply her name. "The story I told Mrs. Baggot was a lot of rot. But I had to lie to her. You see, my work is secret, and Mrs. Baggot is quite a talker."

"What is your work?"

I did not answer at once. Instead, I gave her a swift look, and indulged in some keen-eyed business. I thought it might impress her.

"I'm in the Intelligence Service."

She hesitated. I do not think I had entirely convinced her. But there was reasonable doubt in her eyes. I hurried on to consolidate my advantage.

"You must be reasonable. I've been here five days. If I had any designs on the flat, I would have done whatever it was long ago."

"Mercia" relaxed a little.

"But what are you doing here?" she asked.

After sufficient hesitation, I looked at her as if I were trying to sum her up. Then I appeared to make a decision. I took her close to the window and pointed across at Kalpini's.

"Can you see those two men waiting in that shop? They're detectives—fellow detectives of mine. My job is to watch from this side. You must realize that I can't say more than that!"

That should satisfy her. My air of engaging candour alone was worth the money. But she was intelligent—blast it!

"We can soon find out if that's true," she said. "We'll go across to the shop and ask them."

I gave an easy laugh (not that I felt it).

"I can't do that."

"Why not?"

"I can't tell them I've told you."

"Aren't you eventually going to report my having been here?"

"You don't understand," I said slowly.

"I think I do!"

She went past me towards the door, and for a moment I lost my head. I caught her by the arm; not roughly or anything, in fact I let it go at once, but it was enough. She stopped. My bluff had failed.

"Look here, you can't—" I began, when she went suddenly to the window. It was a casement affair, and opened outwards. Before I could do anything, "Mercia" had undone the catch. Her mouth opened to speak. In another moment the policeman would be coming up the stairs.

"Wait!"

The word was uttered in a hoarse croak that I scarcely recognized as my own voice.

She hesitated, and I moved towards her. I had been looking round desperately, my brain working like mad. There seemed to be just one way to stop her, a crazy, melodramatic way, but there was no choice.

"If you say anything," I said hoarsely, "I'll shoot! Believe me, I mean it!"

On an occasional table, half hidden by a photograph, was the cigarette lighter; the one that looked like a revolver. Passing the table, I put out my hand behind me and picked this up.

I now pointed it at the girl, suggestively fingering the "trigger."

"It's death if I'm caught, so I mean what I say!" I whispered, "that includes Mrs. Baggot as well as yourself."

She said nothing. Her eyes looked at me wonderingly. I think she was surprised rather than frightened. Knowing it was a fake, I half expected her to laugh in my face. But then I've got a keen sense of the ridiculous, and this situation was ridiculous. However, from her point of view it was clearly different. She had reasons to suppose that I was a desperate character; the revolver would not seem out of place.

"Shut the window!"

I did not know if she would obey. I am a lousy actor, and my face must have told her that I was the more nervous of the two. There was a nasty tense moment while our eyes met. Then she shut the window.

Lord knows where I went from here. My only thought had been to save the present, to stop her shouting at that policeman. Now what?

If I went off, she could lean out of the window and yell herself hoarse. It might be possible to take her with me; but the idea of walking through the streets threatening to shoot her if she got out of step was too much. I might shut her up in the kitchen, only that would involve Mrs. Baggot, who would recognize my "revolver" as her cigarette lighter.

"I'm putting this back in my pocket," I said of the revolver, "because I don't want to alarm Mrs. Baggot. I don't think it's necessary to tell you that unless you do exactly as I say, it's going off."

I shoved the lighter in my pocket. "Mercia" had her eyes fixed on me, but said nothing. I am quite convinced that she was not afraid. I think that very few human beings are, when it comes to the point. The chances are that she would have called my bluff if it had not been for Mrs. Baggot.

"We're going to act," I said, "as if you were really Mercia and I were Tony. Try and remember that you are in the company of someone you've been dreaming about for weeks."

I wished she would say something, for I was beginning to feel like a damn fool. I had a crazy desire to pull out the "revolver" and light a cigarette with it. However, Mrs. Baggot saved me from anything so foolish.

There was a discreet cough before she opened the connecting door.

"Now, you two darlings!" she cooed. "You've said enough sweet things to each other! Lunch is ready."

I shall remember that meal for the rest of my life. It was a cross between a farce and a nightmare. I talked the most awful rot, anything to keep the show going. From time to time I threw in a few "dears" at "Mercia," who remained for the most part silent. For the life of me I could not think of what to do next. Lunch would soon be over. Then where did we go?

Mrs. Baggot, of course, was in her element; absolutely bubbling over. She sat there like a high priestess of emotion presiding over a feast of intrigue. It is extraordinary how women can be satisfied with other people's emotions. How content they can be with second-hand thrills.

At first she kept the conversation general, but she was clearly hoping it would take a personal turn. "Mercia" was probably disappointing. The "unhappy wife" sat silent and preoccupied. No doubt our hostess regarded this as being in character, but I felt she expected revelations.

She wanted to be a sympathetic confident; an understanding friend who knew all. It would have been pleasing if her advice had been sought.

No doubt "Mercia's" grave, motionless face suggested possibilities. There was a hint there of untold longings, of unexploited passions. The trouble was that Mrs. Baggot would have liked a little more of the telling, considerably more of the exploitation.

Our hostess fished, hinted, skirted the idea, and finally said to "Mercia":

"You know, my dear, I want you to feel I'm your friend. Mr. Scott—Tony—has told me so much about you that I knew you as soon as I saw you. Even if I hadn't been told, I knew that you were a suffering woman. I am psychic, you know. I realize just what a person is feeling. I can't help it. I just know!"

The speaker shrugged her massive shoulders.

"As soon as you spoke to me I could read you as if you were a book. You seemed to fill the atmosphere with your love. I want you to let me help you. Tell me what I can do!"

Mrs. Baggot threw out her arms. She suggested a self-sacrificing mother bringing the curtain down on act two. It might have been more effective if she had not upset the pepper-pot.

"Mercia" said nothing. I mumbled some gruff thanks.

Eventually even Mrs. Baggot became somewhat dampened by the girl's lack of response. She must have felt like a tennis player serving to an empty court. Evidently she decided that direct questioning would elicit more information.

"How is your little child?" she asked.

"Mercia" was shaken, but she rallied.

"He's very well, thank you."

"*He!* My dear, I thought it was a girl."

I jumped in quickly.

"Mercia always wanted a boy. Even now she thinks of her baby as a boy."

We were getting on to dangerous ground. I had spoken vividly of "Mercia's" home life, and a few questions could destroy that word picture. Besides, the girl might not try to lie. For I had no idea what she was thinking. So I said:

"Don't think me rude, Mrs. Baggot, but Mercia's home life is so sad that she prefers not to think of it."

"Oh, my dear, of course. I'm so sorry."

Mrs. Baggot gave the girl a look of melting sympathy, and turned, reluctantly, to that inevitable topic—the war.

"It will all be over," she pronounced, "by the end of this year. America is making fifty thousand aeroplanes a week for us."

"A year, surely," I interrupted. "And that is what they are *going* to make."

Mrs. Baggot conceded the point.

"A year, is it! Anyway, Hitler won't like it." She looked at me kindly but crushingly. "I have a friend at the Air Ministry, and *I know*. He tells me that the German planes are made of wood and very rarely get home. And there have been food riots in Austria. I know that because I know a woman who used to live in Vienna. Germany can't possibly last another winter; they're short of fats and things. Their bombing won't stop us. When I was in the country one fell next door, but I didn't turn a hair. I was asleep, of course. The Germans are going to use gas next week. I have a friend in Imperial Chemicals; so *I know*!"

She got to her feet.

"Shall we have coffee next door?"

The testing time had come. "Mercia" knew it too. For a moment our eyes met, then she looked away again.

We went into the living-room.

Mrs. Baggot was clearly not sensitive to atmosphere, or other people's feelings. But, by now, even she began to find something unusual in "Mercia's" continued silence. Finally, she asked the girl if she felt unwell. "Mercia" said "No," and the conversation ceased. Then I asked Mrs. Baggot point-blank if she would leave us alone, adding quickly, "I'm afraid there's something worrying Mercia. I know you'll understand."

Mrs. Baggot gave us a compassionate glance and went off, disappointed, to her bedroom. I turned to "Mercia." What I intended doing was risky, but, I think, inevitable.

"Look here," I burst out, "I'm going to tell you the truth. The real truth. Will you listen to me? And give me your word not to do anything until you've heard me out? To begin with," I went on, taking out the cigarette lighter, "this isn't a revolver."

I took out my case and offered a cigarette. She refused. Her dark eyes were on my face as though she were searching for the truth. I took a cigarette and lit it with the lighter. There was a psychological relief in that act. It seemed to iron out the ridiculous aspect of the situation.

Then I told her the truth. All about my arrest, my escape from the flat, the wireless broadcast, and finally about Kalpini's and the cigar clue.

It was impossible to guess what she thought. Her face remained impassive and expressionless. She seemed to be neither surprised nor frightened. Her calm was baffling. I could not tell whether she believed my story or not.

"I know it's difficult for you to believe me," I continued, "but you must admit that there was nothing to stop me from locking you in the bathroom, and then going off. But if I had done that I was stuck. My only hope is to go on keeping watch on Kalpini's. It's my only link with this fellow Carr. For if they catch me, Carr, will be free to do whatever it is they want to stop. You do see that it's my only chance? If you can't trust me completely, why don't you check up on me? You could come here each day. . . . I can only repeat that if I were really guilty I'd have just cleared off."

I paused, everything depended on her reply to my next question.

"Do you believe me?"

Then she said quietly, "Yes, I believe you." Simply, just like that.

Then she smiled. It was like the dawn breaking on a black world. My spirits suddenly soared. I had an irresistible impulse to catch hold of her. As it was, I put out a hand and said, rather ridiculously, "Shall we shake on that?"

Again that smile.

"If you like."

Solemnly we shook hands. And then she gave a little laugh. It swept away my last vestige of doubt.

"But I'm not trusting you completely," she said frankly. "I'm going to check up on you."

She told me about herself. Her name was Penelope Shaw, and she was an actress. At the outbreak of the war she had joined the A.R.P. as a part-time air-raid warden. As we talked there was a nearby explosion. A delayed-action bomb had gone off.

At once Mrs. Baggot's reassuring face appeared at the connecting door. "Don't worry, dears," she said, "it was only a bomb."

CHAPTER VI

PENNY WAS as good as her word. She kept an eye on me, coming round to the flat every day. In return, she made me do an occasional night watch at her A.R.P. post.

One day we were discussing the war and its effects on people's outlook on life.

"You know," she said seriously, "I used to think the stage was everything. I only seemed to be alive when I was in the theatre, 'playing.' But now, nothing has any value since the war."

"Don't you think," I said, "that everyone has worries, and if they haven't they invent them. And then something really big like the war comes along, and we realize how petty all our little fears and squabbles are?"

"Yes, I expect the war has pulled a lot of us out of that sort of thing. It must bring tremendous spiritual help to people. That sounds rather silly and pretentious, but I expect you know what I mean. Though, of course, we're all such frightful little egoists, that when it's all over we'll run round looking for our silly little values again."

Her A.R.P. post was in the basement of a garage off Devonshire Street, not far from Broadcasting House. I never went there until after dark, usually taking the eight to midnight or the midnight to sixteen hours watch (the most unpopular one amongst the Wardens). There was little chance of my being recognized, especially since Penny had introduced me as an old friend.

I enjoyed my brief stay working amongst those Wardens, ordinary men and women who faced terror raining from the skies, joked rather self-consciously about what they called their funk holes; fought fires, saved lives—and often died.

My break with the post came suddenly. I was with Penny watching from the flat window, when, at eleven forty-five a.m., on April the 3rd, 1941, a girl walked into Kalpini's. She was flaxen-haired, about twenty, dressed in a white coat. Something was said, and the assistant reached out for a box of Pagani's black cigars.

As the assistant took this down he dislodged an adjacent box, which fell to the floor. This was probably the arranged signal; for one of the detectives got to his feet.

I was in a quandary. Clearly, it would be fatal for me to go down, announce myself, and suggest that the girl should be arrested. Because, apart from the fact that she might be quite innocent, it would merely result in my being detained, with the police satisfied that they had got Carr.

I watched through the binoculars to see what the detectives would do. They made no immediate move, so I concluded that they intended to follow the flaxen-haired girl. This was one hell of a situation. They would go off into the blue, leaving me in the dark as to what happened.

"I can't go," I said to Penny, "but do you think you could follow the girl?"

"I should think so."

"I'm sorry to have to ask you, and I'm damned if I know what you can do, except to try and find out where she lives. . . . You'll have to be careful of the police."

Penny gave a little chuckle, and went out of the flat.

In Kalpini's the assistant was counting out the change. When she got this, the flaxen-haired girl came out of the shop and turned towards Piccadilly. A second or two later one of the detectives followed. I could see Penny on my own side of the street, almost level with our quarry. In this order they proceeded down Bond Street. Soon they were out of my sight.

Relaxing with an uneasy sigh, I lit a cigarette. God knows what would emerge from it all. I had to rely on luck and Penny's intelligence.

It is extraordinary how slowly time goes when you are awaiting news. For the past few days I had, found myself drifting; the whole thing had become rather unreal. Satisfied that I was doing all that was possible, it had ceased to worry me. But now the race had started.

I paced up and down the flat, chain-smoking. Ages seemed to pass, though, actually, Penny was back in less than two hours. I let her in, searching her face for information. With a wry smile she threw her hat into a chair.

"What happened?"

"Let me have a cigarette," she said; and when I had given her this, "I don't know if my news is good or bad—we both lost her."

"Oh, Lord!"

"We turned into Piccadilly towards Hyde Park, and then we walked along on the Ritz side of the street."

"Were you behind the detective?"

"No, I was in between, feeling rather like part of a procession. Anyway, when we got to the traffic lights near Green Park Station the girl suddenly got into a taxi, which went off as the lights went green."

"What did the detective do?"

"We couldn't do anything. There wasn't another taxi there."

"Damn!" I gave Penny a look. "What have you been doing since?"

"I waited until another taxi came along and took it."

I was surprised.

"Where to?"

She tilted up her face and gave me an amused smile.

"Harrods."

I began to feel rather hopeful about the outcome of this story. Penny was looking too pleased for it to be otherwise. Besides, the time she was taking over the telling of it suggested a happy ending.

"All right," I said, "you've done something clever. How did you know she was going to Harrods?"

"When I was walking behind the girl I noticed that she was wearing new shoes. And I knew that she had bought them this morning, because she had a Harrods bag under her arm—where she had probably put her old pair. She was limping a bit, and she stopped twice to ease one of the shoes."

"Would Harrods send a woman out with shoes too tight?" I asked.

"My angel, don't you know that it is woman's vanity always to ask for half a size smaller than they take!"

"Did she go back to Harrods to have it eased?"

Penny nodded, and a whistle of admiration escaped me.

"That's damn good. Then what?"

"I waited, and followed her out. In the Brompton Road she asked the doorman to get her a taxi."

"Did you follow it?"

"No. There wasn't another cab, so I asked the doorman what address "my friend" had gone to."

"What was the address?"

"Notting Hill Underground Station. . . . took a cab there, but I'm afraid I didn't see her again."

I took a turn round the room. Penny was right; she had said she did not know if her news was good or bad. Neither did I. But we had got somewhere. Flaxen-haired had gone to Notting Hill Station (probably to avoid giving her real address). The public-house where I had been arrested was in Kensington High Street, roughly half a mile from Notting Hill. It began to look as though flaxen-haired really was Carr's agent, and that my double lived in the Notting Hill district.

"What are you going to do?" asked Penny.

"I'm going to have a sniff round Notting Hill."

"What about the police?"

"I'll have to chance them."

I got Penny to give me her telephone number, and I promised to keep in touch.

"I'm taking a risk letting my one and only spy-suspect get away," she smiled. "And what about Mrs. Baggot? She'll be heart-broken!"

"Tell her I did the decent thing and sent you back to your husband and child."

A detective was still at Kalpini's, presumably waiting for instructions. I slipped out of the flat and walked quickly towards Oxford Street. The Central London Line took me from Bond Street to that rather mixed neighbourhood—Notting Hill.

My plan was very vague, just to walk about hoping that I would see flaxen-haired. I left the shopping centre round the station and wandered down Holland Park Avenue, and round a place called Ladbroke Square, with its large houses now reduced to the status of cheap flats. Then, turning back, I strolled up a hill past the tower of a waterworks, guarded by what looked like a machine-gun post.

After some hours, I realized that this aimless wandering was ridiculous, and I had a meal in a tea-shop. Then I went back to Notting Hill Underground Station; people were hurrying back from their work, with that "let's-get-home-quick-look" that seemed so prevalent in war-torn London. I hung about for some time, and got a suspicious look from the lift attendant. To squash this, I casually mentioned that I was waiting for my wife. He understood then.

Nine o'clock came, and the light had faded from the sky. There seemed to be no point in waiting any longer. I decided to stay another fifteen minutes—just for luck.

A lift came up and discharged its cargo of passengers. I was standing by a ticket machine, underneath a subdued light, as the small group of people went past me. In the rear was a girl with a white coat and a Robin-hood hat. Her head was bent down, but as she came abreast of me she looked up.

It was flaxen-haired.

For a moment we looked into each other's face. I had a feeling that I was gaping like an idiot. Then she went out into the street.

I had found her! But it was so surprising, that it required a mental kick before I moved after her. Fortunately her white coat made her a conspicuous figure. She did not appear to be in any hurry. She went round a corner and there waited at a bus stop. Standing on the edge of the pavement, with head down and hands thrust into her pockets, she appeared to be wholly preoccupied with her thoughts. I went past in the darkness and stood in a doorway, watching.

She got on a No. 52 bus. I was about to do the same, when I spotted a disengaged taxi held up by the traffic lights.

I told the driver to let the bus pass and then to follow it.

I could see flaxen-haired sitting in the bus, still apparently lost in thought. I was puzzled to know where she was going. We had left the Notting Hill district (where I assumed Carr lived), and it was difficult to account for her movements. What station had she come from when she came out of the Underground? Where was she going now? Possibly she intended meeting Carr at some prearranged spot.

In the darkness we passed Kensington Court, and went along by the park. The same route over which I had travelled with Wicket and his haddocks. Then, at a stop near the Wellington Barracks, flaxen-haired got off and began walking down the slope towards Knightsbridge.

I paid the driver and set off after the girl. Again she was walking leisurely. When we had gone about fifty yards she stopped near a sort of alley-way, and tapped on a door. This opened. There was a faint glow of subdued light and she went inside. The door shut again.

I went up to the door. It was a double affair with an awning overhead. I hung about for a moment, undecided. It might be a mistake to knock before knowing more about the place. A fellow in the Air Force came up, and I tackled him.

"What's this place?"

"The Wellington Club."

"Can I get in?"

"Only if you're a member, old lad."

"I'm not."

"Well, I am. I'll sign you in."

He knocked on the door, said "Good evening, Bill" to the porter who opened it, and we stepped inside. Behind a cubbyhole was a page who took our hats and coats. Then we went down some steps, past gold-tinted walls and through a curtain into the club. A burst of swing music, lights and laughter greeted us. There were pictures of cabaret turns on the decorated walls, and a balcony that looked down on to the dance floor and bar. The place was full, mostly with men in uniform.

"Coming down for a drink?" asked my host.

"No. I think I'll stay up here, thanks."

Flaxen-haired had shed her coat and hat, and now, drink in hand, she was standing by the bar.

She was rather above medium height, slim and blonde. Her cheekbones were high, and, I do not know why, she gave the impression of using but little make-up. Her face appeared wistful, somewhat sad. But her main characteristic seemed to be passivity. All her movements were unhurried. I have never seen anyone stand so still.

She looked down at the floor and not at the scene about her.

This suggested a detachment of spirit, as though she were unaware of the music, chatter and noise of the club. She did not appear to be English. If anything, she looked as though she came from one of the Scandinavian countries.

I found myself tapping a foot to the beat of the syncopated music. There was such an air of life about the crowded room that my grim watch seemed rather unreal. A dark-haired waitress with prominent eyes, and two waiters, were serving drinks and food at the tables. There was tobacco smoke, noise and the clink of glasses. The plumpish, cheerful man at the piano was singing, "If you want it, you've got to buy it, 'cos we don't give nothing away," into the microphone, using a lyrical version of his own. Everyone seemed to be smiling.

If Carr came in, I meant to have a show-down on the spot. I was going to tackle him, yell for waiters, managers and the whole Air Force and tell them to hold us both until the police arrived.

Then flaxen-haired put down her glass, and began moving gracefully past the dancing couples towards the balcony. I edged away, so as to have two people between myself and the top of the steps. She came up these, and went through the curtain leading to the stairs and street. There was a telephone there, so it looked as though she were going to use it.

I moved back towards the curtain, hoping to hear what was said. Unfortunately the noise was too loud. It was risky to wait there, so I went to the end of the balcony.

In a short while flaxen-haired returned and went down to the cloakroom. It looked as though the meeting was off. But there was just a chance that she had arranged a rendezvous elsewhere.

I went quickly up the stairs, got my hat and coat, and passed into the night.

I hailed a taxi to stand by, got in, let down the window, and waited. Soon a dim white-coated figure came out of the Club. She came towards my cab, and I shrunk back.

"Are you engaged?"

"I am. Sorry, miss."

There was a faint trace of some foreign accent in her speech that was not unattractive. Though spoke softly, she enunciated, as foreigners often do, very clearly. Soon she got another cab.

"Notting Hill Station."

She got in. The door slammed, and her taxi turned in the direction of Kensington.

"Go to Notting Hill Station, as fast as you can!" I told my driver.

We also turned and began moving quickly through the night. Soon we passed flaxen-haired's cab, and I peered out of the oval window at the back. The two dim lights were visible behind us for some time.

Dismissing the cab at the station, I waited in the shadows, thankful that there were so few people about. Soon a taxi drew up. Flaxen-haired got out and began walking slowly in the direction of Holland Park. I let her go ahead for about thirty yards, and then followed. Visibility was good enough to enable me to pick her out at this range.

On a very dark night there is a technique for blackout walking. If you look up you can see the glow of the sky and the outline of buildings, this enables you to steer a course.

The girl crossed the road, continued for some way, and then took a turning left. When I got there I recognized it as the road leading to the water tower. Soon flaxen-haired stopped outside a house, and fumbled in her handbag.

My heart raced. Perhaps Carr was in that dark building.

My quarry began moving down some area steps and dis-appeared from view. I stood quite still for a few seconds, a glow of elation warming me—the sort of feeling that comes to a gambler when he sees his horse first past the post.

I gave flaxen-haired a couple of minutes to get inside, and then went softly forward and down the steps. From the area window came faint chinks of light escaping through the black-out curtains. I crept on tiptoe lest any noise betrayed me. There was a bell-push on the door, but no nameplate or card. However, I got the number, 152A, which suggested that it was a flat.

Then I turned to go.

There was the lightest of light footsteps at my side. Someone had come out from behind the area steps.

"Good evening, Mr. Stephen!" said a man's voice.

Something was pressed into my side, and a torch was flashed on. The diffused light showed me that the "something" was an ugly, squat automatic.

CHAPTER VII

THEY HAD LAID a trap, and I had walked right into it. For a moment it occurred to me that it might be the police. Then I realized that this was nonsense. The man behind me was Carr.

"Shall we go in?"

He spoke in perfect English, and very naturally, as though he were inviting a friend in for a drink. This casualness disarmed me. It seemed slightly ridiculous to offer resistance in the face of such nonchalance (not that I could have done anything against that automatic).

When he opened the door I stepped inside.

"Would you mind putting on the light?" he said. "It's just on your left. . . . It's all right, it's shaded."

Feeling like someone in a dream, I did so, and a subdued light lit a carpeted passage. My companion shut the door, and motioned me down the narrow hall-way.

"Second door on the left."

Momentarily bereft of all initiative, I went into the room indicated. It was a living-room, cheaply furnished and typical of thousands of London's more modest flats. Flaxen-haired was standing there, still wearing her white coat. Her face was expressionless.

The man behind me gave a good-natured chuckle.

"When Chrissa recognized you at Notting Hill Station, she got quite a shock—especially when you followed her. It'd be interesting to know how you knew her. Still, we'll discuss that later. Unlike most women, she went to that Club to give herself time to think. Then she telephoned me. Naturally, I told her to bring you here. . . . You'd better sit down."

I turned to him. Confound it! Why did he have to be so self-possessed and casual. He stood there, automatic in hand, as though it were the most natural thing in the world to usher in a guest at the point of a gun.

He was like me; there was no doubt about that. I should say that he was older—about thirty-eight. His hair, a shade lighter than mine, was inclined to curl. His face seemed fuller, and his complexion was, I think, darker; but the main features appeared to be identical. His assured personality, however, was stronger than mine, and I could not claim to have the same intelligent look in my eyes.

He smiled and—as if reading my thoughts—said: "Yes, we are alike, which is fortunate for me. . . . But go on—sit down. You know, we have quite a lot to talk about. How did you get away from the police? And was it coincidence that brought you to Notting Hill?"

"I don't propose to discuss the matter!"

I spoke coldly and sulkily. He gave me a look that was chiding but not unkind. It made me feel rather childish.

"You were waiting for someone. It would be interesting to know who. Or had you traced me this far? . . . No—I doubt that. But you did know Chrissa? How?" His intelligent eyes searched my face. Then he shrugged his shoulders good-humouredly. "However, you don't wish to discuss it."

He looked at the automatic in his hand.

"I think it would be easier if I didn't have to wave this at you. If you agree, I suggest that I tie you to a chair. Don't you think that would solve the problem?"

He seemed to ask me in all earnestness, and, having regained my temper, I could not resist a smile.

"I think it might."

"Chrissa," he said, "after you take off your coat, would you see if there's any rope or cord?"

"I think there's some in the kitchen."

She went off.

"Get something strong," Carr called out after her. He gave a tolerant smile. "Women are apt to under-estimate things on an occasion like this." Then, quite unexpectedly, "Is it cold out?"

"Not very," I smiled.

"I haven't been out since the day you were arrested."

I began to catch something of his detached spirit, and found myself saying, "Were you going to meet that fellow in the raincoat in that pub?"

He nodded.

"But luckily I was late. Curious coincidence that you should go there just at that time. What would you say the odds were of that happening again—several millions to one?"

"Why do the police want you?"

He was quite unabashed at the question.

"I'm German, you know. Not unnaturally you want your country to win." A gleam came into his eyes, a fanatic's look. It was only there for a second, but it seemed to show me his soul. He added softly, "That's how I feel about mine."

We fell silent. We had touched on something deep and divergent between us. He was a spy, working against England. Despite this, I do not know that I hated him personally. Had it been possible, of course, I would have destroyed him, as one destroys a pest. But I could not help realizing that at least he was a patriot. He faced, unflinchingly, it seemed, the risk of a firing squad; and every day endured the very danger from the skies that he was helping to bring down on England.

In a moment or two he smiled, as though ashamed of that glimpse of emotionalism. He said—lightly, "Yes, we are like two opponents in a cricket team. We each want to win. That's something you English are very fond of—sport!"

I said nothing. A vision of wrecked houses and lives, of mangled bodies and tears, of German hate and brutality, rose before me.

Chrissa came back with some cord.

"I hope that's not too tight," said Carr, as he tied me to a chair.

When he had finished, I had one arm bound to the chair, but the other was relatively free.

"Would you like something to eat?" asked my host.

"I don't think so, thanks."

"I should. We usually have something—though it's rather late to-night."

Chrissa went out to the kitchen. In a few minutes she returned. She had put on an apron and looked like any other housewife.

"I think I'd better open a tin of something. There's not very much steak," she said.

I resented that remark. The truth was that this matter-of-fact atmosphere offended my sense of the dramatic.

"Chrissa can usually get something extra," said Carr, "that's the advantage of being a woman; they're able to charm things from people as important as butchers."

They were like a respectable married couple, chatting over their marketing troubles. If this talk went on, I would not have been surprised to find myself asking Carr how his flowers had come up the previous year.

Their attitude was not a pose. But beneath all this lay a serious problem: Carr had got me into the house because he had some plan. It was clear that I was either going to be of some use to him—or else be eliminated.

Chrissa went to the door; from here she gave Carr a quick look, and then glanced at me. Carr's face remained impassive, but he gave the slightest of slight nods. Whatever it was—my fate had been decided.

I tried to decide what I would do were I in his shoes. It was difficult to guess. He looked calm and studious. You could not but feel that he would deprecate any form of personal violence. Despite the broadness of his shoulders and the strength of his face, there was something of the ascetic about him.

I wondered whether he and Chrissa were married. It was obvious that she adored him. She would sit impassively still, but her eyes followed him when he moved. She was so graceful, so meek and wistful, that it gave you a curious thrill to think of the passionate fire burning in her fragile body.

As these musings passed through my mind, I glanced round the room. The furniture was very ordinary; two arm-chairs and a divan sprinkled with cushions, a cheap wireless set on which lay a copy of the *Radio Times*.

"What are you going to do with me?" I asked.

Carr smiled.

"Suppose we eat first, and worry about that—afterwards. Anyway, I haven't made up my mind."

Then we talked of the War—and Germany.

I found him a curious mixture. He possessed a sense of humour; and, I think, a feeling of tolerance, both unusual traits in a German. Despite these characteristics, he remained a fanatic. He believed in his leader's dreams, though they might fly in the face of all human ethics, and that made him a dangerous man.

Casually, I asked him why the police were so anxious to take him. I mentioned that I suspected some connection with the Admiralty. And, just as casually, he told me: "You have a new anti-submarine device. And we got hold of it."

I listened intently to what he said. Then, as if reading my thoughts, he gave a reproving smile.

"You must not think me so stupid, Mr. Stephen, as to tell you something that your Admiralty does not already know."

Chrissa came in with a tray, and Carr helped her to lay the table. We sat down to eat. The girl was silent; perhaps she did not regard the situation with the same equanimity as her lover. He gently chided her.

"She goes to the Coronet Cinema and is greatly attracted by the American heroes. Who is it this week—Robert Taylor?"

She smiled at his foolishness, but said nothing.

"There they go!"

Carr paused to listen. Aeroplanes were flying overhead. Presumably German ones. I expected them to show some signs of exultation. Instead, they reacted, like most Londoners.

"The sirens haven't gone," said Chrissa.

"Don't they seem low to-night!"

Then came the sound of distant bombing, and the wail of the sirens. We continued to eat.

Carr was discussing the propaganda effect of films, when we heard a swishing, whistling sound. It was a bomb dropping from some five miles up. Death was falling, swiftly, ruthlessly. It made you very conscious of living. The walls of the dimly-lit room pressed around you; for a moment you hated the gloom, you felt stifled.

When we had finished the meal, Chrissa made some coffee, but Carr, fetching two glasses and a bottle of whiskey, said, smiling, "We are not on a hen party, you know!"

He poured off a stiff whiskey for me and one for himself. The thought crossed my mind that he might want to get me drunk in the hope that I would talk. This did not worry me. I have a good head for drink.

The girl had taken out the rest of the dishes, and I lifted my glass with my free hand. My companion, seated on the other side of the table, did likewise. He was examining his cigarette. He did not look at me.

I sipped the whiskey.

My palate happens to be very sensitive, and it warned me that there was something besides Scotch in that glass. I glanced quickly at Carr, who was still studiously occupied. A grim smile flittered across my face. He would probably have got away with it in ninety-nine cases out of a hundred. . . . This was the hundredth.

It so happened that once in Shanghai I had met an affable Russian. We had tasted the night life together, drunk a great deal—and finished up in a haunt of his choosing. . . . Chinese girls, smoke and a jazz band. Almond eyes smiling. The Russian had himself carried over our drinks from the bar; down went mine in one gulp. Soon the room had become a haze—then darkness. When I recovered, the affable Russian had gone, and so had my wallet. Ship's surgeon suggested butyl had been used. Whatever it was, I had never forgotten the taste.

Carr's studied indifference was understandable now.

I looked quickly round the room. There was no water. So I said, "Do you think I could have some water in this whiskey?"

"I'm so sorry. Of course . . . Chrissa!"

There was no reply, and he went out to the kitchen. With my free hand I chucked the contents of my glass into an empty brass flower-vase, and then poured out some more whiskey. Carr had drunk some of his, so the dope had been in my glass—not in the bottle.

He came back with some water in a jug, and added some to my whiskey. I drunk it down at one go. He gave a light sigh of relief. I was uncertain just how soon the dope was supposed to work, and I'm not much of an actor.

He sat down, and we went on talking. After a bit, I let my voice grow hoarse; then my head flopped on to my chest. I shut my eyes. Soon he came over to me. His hands touched my head, forcing it back. When he prised open one of my eyelids I rolled up my eyes. Apparently he was satisfied. Going to the door, he called for Chrissa.

"Is it all right?" she whispered.

"You need not whisper—he is unconscious."

They were speaking in German, a language I understand. They did not raise their voices, but every word was clear. There was now more urgency in Carr's voice.

"You must pack," he said. "Leave nothing!"

He came back into the room. I heard him moving about. Evidently he was removing anything that he considered incriminating. I was in an agony of mind lest he discover the doped whiskey in the flower-vase. Finally he undid the rope which bound me.

There was the sound of something being splashed into my glass. After some time I heard the girl's voice: "I think I've got everything."

"I'll see."

Carr left the room, presumably to make certain. When he came back they stood whispering in the hall-way. Sometimes I missed a few words, but on the whole I got most of it. My main hope was that they would mention their destination; unfortunately, they did not do so.

They were talking about some addresses.

"Can you remember them?" said the man.

"I've written them down."

Carr gave a "tck" of annoyance.

"My dear, I've told you to memorize everything. Never write anything unless you must."

"I was afraid of getting it wrong," she said, in her soft, sweet voice. "You said it was important."

"All the more reason for keeping it in your head. Where have you written it down?"

"It's in my bag . . . here."

"Now you must get this into your head, my dear. If something should happen to me, you will have to do everything. I'll read them to you."

I listened, scarcely able to believe my luck. It was fortunate that Carr, the more intelligent and dominant of the two, should of his nature wish to instruct her. Nine out of ten men would have let her read for herself.

Carr slowly read out: "A. Caldecott, 917b, Old Kent Road, London. . . . A. T. Pennington, The Post Office, Prestby, near Market Bosney, Lincolnshire. . . . R. Bryant, Pin Down Farm, Cradstone, near Leicester. . . . The Post Office one must be marked 'to be called for.' I'll repeat them before I destroy them."

He did so—three times.

"I've already posted the letter to Caldecott," said Chrissa. "Is it really necessary to do it this way?"

"Certainly. If anyone is caught, they cannot betray the rest."

"Will you have it in time?"

"Unless something goes wrong."

"What about the terms?"

"They're fixed."

I strained my ears lest they missed something important.

"I suppose it will get through all right?" said the girl.

"I think so. You see, England will have music."

I found myself mentally repeating Chrissa's remark, "Will you have it in time?" Had "it" been the object of the police search of my person at Scotland Yard? . . . "You see, England will have music." What did that mean?

"Now, you can telephone," said Carr.

"What is the number?"

"Whitehall 1212."

I nearly betrayed myself with a cry of surprise. They were telephoning Scotland Yard!

A sound of someone dialling, then: "I want to speak to someone in connection with Michael Stephen," said Chrissa, "the police broadcast a message a little while ago. . . . Thank you."

She began to whisper that they were getting someone, but Carr silenced her with a warning "ssh." Soon she was saying: "I have a message to deliver concerning Michael Stephen. Am I talking to the right gentleman?" Evidently assured, she continued: "If you will send someone to 152, Campden Hill Gardens, you will find him in the basement flat. . . . No, I am afraid I cannot tell you who I am. . . . No, I am sorry . . ."

Through half-closed eyelids I watched the couple. The girl put her hand over the mouthpiece of the telephone and said, softly, "They won't believe I am serious."

Carr gave an indulgent smile.

"I expect they have a lot of false alarms. But they will come."

"What shall I say?"

"Tell them you had helped Stephen—but got frightened. You can say that he is now drunk."

Chrissa repeated this. When she had replaced the receiver, the couple moved into the next room. Soon I heard Carr say in answer to a question of the girl's: "No, my dear, we cannot take it. You must leave it. It will be all right."

Footsteps in the hall; the front door slammed. They had gone. I opened my eyes. The electric light was still on. My glass and a nearby empty bottle of whiskey remained (Carr had evidently poured most of it away).

I would have to hurry if I was going to follow them. Visibility was just about right for tailing—bright enough to see them, but sufficiently dark to enable one to merge in the shadows.

I was about to go to the door, when a noise made me pause.

A faint shuffling sound was coming from the next room. I smiled grimly. Carr was a very thorough gentleman. He was making sure that I really was unconscious. The slamming of the flat door had been a blind. So obligingly I slumped back in my chair, expecting that my double would creep back to reassure himself.

Sitting there, I could but admire the simplicity of his manoeuvres. By turning me over to the police, as he hoped, he left the field free for himself. A few minutes passed. I strained my ears listening for other sounds, but there was nothing. It was puzzling. Carr could not afford to wait too long, for the police must soon arrive. I decided to give it another ten seconds. At that moment the shuffling noise was repeated— very faintly. It sounded like someone shifting their weight from one leg to another.

I remained in the chair, my half-closed eyes fixed on the door. This was slightly ajar, and the glimpse of dark passage looked ominous. I pictured Carr waiting outside, gun in hand, his nerves tense as he listened for some sound from me.

I have too much imagination for this waiting game, and decided to have a go for him. I went on tiptoe towards the door, my body braced, my heart thumping in my chest. Reaching the electric switch I flicked out the light and dropped to the floor. I expected some move from Carr—but nothing happened. Then, on my hands and knees, I began crawling up the passage. It was pitch black and progress was of necessity slow, because it was essential not to give away my position.

As I waited for a possible shot, I heard a repetition of the noise. This was in the next room, and sent me edging towards it. My hand went out and cautiously pushed open the door.

I waited for a second or two, and then went into the room. It was as dark as the passage.

But where was Carr? It seemed strange that he made no move. The door had creaked as it swung open, making my heart race. Groping blindly, I crawled on—searching for him. My hand found a chair, and, as I felt cautiously round this, the noise came again. It sounded exactly in front of me. Then I got a shock. Something brushed past me, something that was soft and frolicksome; and made me curse like mad.

It was a cat.

This is what Carr had told Chrissa to leave behind. This was the cause of the noise that had kept me like a fool in that chair.

I got up and went back to the living-room. Here I collected my hat and the binoculars, switched out the light again and groped my way to the flat door. I wanted to get out—quick. As my fingers touched the door-knob there came a sound from outside.

Some men were coming down the area steps.

CHAPTER VIII

I WENT BACK up the passage, noiselessly and quickly. Unfortunately, the lay-out was strange to me, and it was impossible to see a thing in the dark. The police were knocking on the door as I reached a room at the end of the passage. My groping fingers found a kitchen table, and from there I worked towards the wall.

I brushed against a dresser, piled with crockery, and fell into a cold sweat—I had nearly knocked over a jug. There was a stove and a sink, and then hands touched a cloth and a chair.

I had to move with agonizing slowness. The place was full of things that, if upset, would make the dickens of a clatter. It was like a nightmare groping round that dark room—searching for a way out.

Behind me, the police had flashed on a torch. There came a tinkling sound as one of the glass panes of the door was smashed. In a few seconds a hand would come through this aperture and open the door.

Then, between the dresser and the sink, I discovered the back door. By some merciful Providence this opened noiselessly. Possibly Carr had oiled it for just such an emergency as this.

I found myself in a gravel patch surrounded by a low wall topped with trellis-work. There was no time to be lost, so I went over the wall—quickly. Here was another gravel patch, not unlike the one I had left. A cat sped away as I made for the next partitioning wall, but there was no sign of a human being, nor any noise from the houses. My idea being to get as far away from the police as possible, I did not trouble about my direction. I went across more backyards before thinking about trying to get out. Then, as I was crossing yet another tiny garden, something brought me up with a start. It was a man saying, "Did you want any place in particular, cock?"

I turned, a nasty feeling in my stomach, and tried to bluff it out.

"Sorry to come in like this," I said, "but I've been locked out of my place. I was trying to get in the back."

"Where are you from? Next door?"

"That's right."

"Number one?"

"Yes."

He came out from the shadows, taking a pipe from his mouth. "That's interesting, cock; number one's the other part of the street!"

I braced myself, ready to fight, wondering whether I could land a strong enough punch to knock him cold. Apparently unconcerned about my lie, he tapped his pipe against the side of his shoe.

"Are you running away from someone?"

"Good Lord, no!"

My tone was a mixture of carelessness and surprise. In reply, he turned towards the back door.

"In that case, you'd better hide in here."

There was nothing much one could say to that.

I followed him into the kitchen, which was a mass of unwashed crockery and empty tins. Clearly my host was a bachelor. We went into a sitting-room strewn with newspapers and copies of *The Statesman* and *Tribune*.

My host was about thirty-four or five, very lean, with black untidy hair, a wisp of which fell over his forehead. He wore thick glasses. I expected him to cross-question me; instead, he reached out for a bottle.

"Here's some stuff that tastes like furniture polish, but has sherry marked on the bottle. You can have some, if you like, but I accept no responsibility." He splashed some of it into two glasses. "We might drink it on the grounds that its effects may obliterate the taste."

He adjusted his glasses, which had a habit of falling down, and began to talk—and talk, and talk. He had left wing ideas and wanted conscription of capital as the solution to winning the War. But he did not really wish to convince me, he merely wished to talk.

"I think this communal feeding's a good thing, cock. Everybody ought to get together, instead of not speaking unless they're introduced. It's the separation of people that causes wars. If everybody shared things, they wouldn't be so possessive, and eventually that spirit would spread to the nations. . . . Personally, I volunteered for the Army, but only on the grounds that you're reasonably certain to eat there!"

He talked for hours. This, I realized, was the price I paid for his protective hospitality. Sitting there, with his eyes staring at me through his thick lenses, he was like a black spider that has caught a victim in his web. I thought of the names and addresses that Carr had made Chrissa memorize. In the morning I would investigate the London one.

"A. Caldecott, 917b, Old Kent Road." The words ran through my head, mixed up with the steady drone

from my companion. . . . Who was Caldecott? Was he
a German spy? If so, what would I do?

I yawned. Words flowed at me and over me. Nothing is so tiring as listening. Soon I slept.

* * * * *

Next morning my host gave me breakfast, more
talk and a reluctant farewell. There was no sign of
the police, and gratefully I caught a bus to the Elephant and Castle. As I walked down the long shabby
thoroughfare that is the Old Kent Road, I felt that at
least there was something upon which to work. A Caldecott—whoever he might be—suggested possibilities.

Number 917b proved to be a Newspaper shop,
dingy and small. Windows on the upper floor had
been damaged by bomb blast, and were boarded
up. The place told me nothing; so, with my hat well
down on my head, I crossed the road and looked into
the window. This was full of newspapers, magazines
and cheap paper-covered books, with a few sidelines
such as aspirin cards and corn cures. But there was
no name above the shop, no hint of what Caldecott's
connection with the establishment might be.

I did not know what to do, until I saw something
that gave me an idea; a faded notice in the window
bore the legend, "Letters can be addressed here. Price
one penny." I came to a snap decision, and stepped
into the dingy interior of the shop. If my plan came
unstuck I could always run for it.

A young girl aged about ten came out from the
back room. She was freckled, extremely dirty, but
wearing an enormous grin.

"Is there a letter for A. Caldecott?" I asked.

"'Oo?"

"Caldecott."

She could not get it, so she turned and picked out a bundle of letters from an old toffee tin.

"You 'ave a look for yourself."

I took the bundle. The second letter was addressed to A. Caldecott; it was typewritten. I put it in my pocket. The rest of the letters, together with a penny, I handed back to the girl. I gave a sigh of relief.

"Why aren't you evacuated to the country?" I asked.

"We wus. But mum didn't like leaving London. An' if a bomb 'its yer on the nut, you ain't got a nut, that's all. You don't want ter worry."

On this note of profound philosophy, I left. In a neighbouring public-house I read—with dismay—the contents of the envelope. This consisted of a slip of paper on which was typed: "9.4.41. Wat. 4.4 H.5. 9½."

My heart sank. It told me nothing. The first part was clearly a date—April 9th, 1941. But the rest was, to me, meaningless. If it was a code, it was too short a message to be read. There was nothing for it but to visit the other two addresses. For they might have something better to offer. To ensure that Carr continued to use the Old Kent Road address (and did not alter his plan), I decided to post the message back to Caldecott. With luck, he might never know that it had been opened; certainly, the girl had not got the name right.

In the city I bought some envelopes, found a shop that sold typewriters, and on the pretext of wanting to buy one, typed out Caldecott's address. After posting this, I decided that Pin Down Farm, near Leicester, would be my next objective. April 9th, 1941. It looked as though something important was going to happen on that day. It was now April the 4th, which left me five days to get some results. It was useless trying to formulate plans. I would have to deal with events as they occurred. Perhaps Pin Down Farm would provide a meeting with R. Bryant, whoever he might be.

During the train journey to Leicester, I looked at the piece of paper on which I had jotted down the message: "9.4.41. Wat. 4.4. H.5. 9½."

It still did not mean a thing to me.

CHAPTER IX

AT LEICESTER, following the directions of a porter, I caught a bus from the Centre, and jolted out of the industrial town into green country. Shortly after passing a place called Syston, I got off. Cradstone, it seemed, was some two miles from the main road.

I walked between hedgerows, enjoying the first taste of spring. Cattle grazed peacefully in the pastures, but signposts had been taken down, and here and there a cart in a field reminded one of the threat of enemy parachute troops.

Then I caught up with a fellow walking beside a horse and cart. My story was that I was an insurance agent. The big towns had become hopeless risks, and we were prospecting the country. Casually, I mentioned Pin Down Farm. It was, he informed me, a mile beyond Cradstone, but he could tell me nothing about its occupants.

Leaving my companion at the hamlet of Cradstone, I went on alone. Soon I left the road and got through a quickthorn hedge. I wanted to reconnoitre the farm before taking any action. In front of me was a thickly wooded hillock, and in a few minutes I was moving amidst oak and beech trees. I reached the summit of the rise. Below me was a patchwork of English countryside; and there, nestling in a hollow, was Pin Down Farm. I got out my binoculars to have a closer view of it.

Pin Down Farm was a pretentious name for so small a dwelling. For this place was little better than a small cottage. It had a stucco front and a corrugated roof, the whole being boxed in by a square hedge. In the front were flower and vegetable beds, some apple trees and a cedar. In the rear was an outhouse and a chicken-run. Neat white curtains hung at the windows, and some sort of creeper grew round the porch. It all looked innocent enough, very rural and English.

I was getting bored with watching, when the back door of the cottage opened. A woman came out. She was elderly, grey-haired and dressed in black. She threw some scraps to the hens, and then turned back to the house.

I was puzzled. What sort of a place was this? Was it an observation post for the German Intelligence? If so, why in this secluded spot?

By five-thirty it seemed a good idea to get back to Cradstone for a drink. Then an elderly man, who had been cycling along the road, stopped at Pin Down Farm, opened the wicket-gate and wheeled his bike up the gravel path. The woman greeted him with a kiss. They looked like a typical Darby and Joan couple.

I cut back the way I had come and walked along the road towards the house. The wicket-gate opened to my touch. A few moments later, with a feeling of anticipation, I was knocking on the door of Pin Down Farm.

The woman opened it. She had a round, gentle face and kind eyes. She spoke in a soft voice, and looked like that grey-haired mother you hear of in songs. I took a bold line, keeping to my story that I was an insurance agent. Probably I was walking right into trouble. But it seemed the only way. Finesse is all very well when you've time on your hands; I hadn't.

"Does Mr. Bryant live here?" I asked.

"I'm so sorry. I'm afraid he's not here just now."

I hit the bottom with a thud. I don't know whether it was relief or disappointment.

"Does he usually live here?"

"He's been lodging with us for some weeks. He's been gone about two days; but he'll be back."

An idea occurred to me. "My firm wrote to him. I wonder if he got our letter. Only you know what it is with the bombing, sometimes letters go astray."

"There is a letter for him."

My game was obvious enough—take a room and get hold of that letter (presumably it was the one posted by Chrissa). I told her that I had insurance calls to make in the neighbourhood, and asked heir to put me up for a night or two.

The room she showed me was neat and tidy, with a picture of the Virgin and Child over the iron bedstead. The chintz curtains at the latticed windows framed a pleasant view of the country.

Then tea in the parlour. A red plush sofa, some china objects that some people bring back from the seaside; a picture of a glen in the Highlands, and one of some birds in flight; there was even waxed fruit on the figured oak sideboard.

Halfway through tea, I remembered my rôle. I gather that a travelling salesman is pretty fly about what he pays for his keep, so I asked her what she charged. She named a price that was ridiculously cheap, and then looked ashamed, as though she would have liked to give me the food. The anxious look on her gentle, tired face, entirely won my heart.

Her husband kept to the kitchen, but after tea they both came in. They sat down shyly, in case I thought they were intruding. He was a good fellow, with a red face, frank and open. He said: "Mother makes very good cakes. I know, I've eaten them for forty years."

"She gave a shy little smile, like a schoolgirl on being complimented before strangers. Soon I got the conversation round to Bryant. I wanted to find out where they kept the letter.

"I suppose the letter waiting for him is from us. Do you think I could see it?"

Crossing to the sideboard, Mrs. Warren pulled open a drawer. She took out a letter and handed it to me. I felt a quickening of my pulse. The address had been typed in on the same machine as the letter to Caldecott.

I did some quick thinking. Then I said: "No, that's not from my firm."

Mrs. Warren put it back in the sideboard drawer, which she did not trouble to lock. It looked as though my task was going to be easier than I had dared hope.

She said: "What a pity, Mr. Scott!" (Scott was the name I had given.) "But if you wanted to see Mr. Bryant very badly, we can tell you he's gone to Horncastle."

"Where's that?" I asked as casually as I could.

"Over past Grantham."

"Do you know where he's staying?"

"I'm afraid we don't. But I understand Horncastle's not a big place."

They looked distressed at not being able to help me.

"I'll be working towards that direction," I said. (Not that I had the least idea where Horncastle might be.) "The trouble is that I don't know what Mr. Bryant looks like."

Mrs. Warren gave a smile.

"We've got a picture of him. Dad snapped him with his camera."

The husband chuckled reminiscently.

"He wouldn't pose for me. Made quite a fuss, didn't he, mother! But I got him when he wasn't looking. When he saw the result, he liked it and wanted all the prints and negative. But I kept one print."

I could understand Mr. Bryant's reluctance to pose. Better still his anxiety to destroy the results. They showed me the snapshot. Bryant was a big fellow, with a strong jaw and well-defined features. Easy to remember.

"If you go to Horncastle," said Mr. Warren, "stay at the Ox-Post. It's run by a man we know. You'll find he'll treat you well."

Then they told me something about themselves. They had been married forty years, and came from London—Streatham way. Warren had worked in the city, in one of those old-fashioned, reliable firms. I could picture him as he left his semi-detached villa every morning. He would have a bowler hat on his head, and under his arm a newspaper. Each year he and the wife went to Clacton or Margate. Sometimes they talked of saving a bit extra and going abroad, but they could never stand the idea of the messed-up food the foreigners gave you to eat! The wife's cooking was good enough for any man—and better for your inside.

Warren took out insurance policies, and paid his debts on the nail. Hard work never killed any man, and he had done his share. The peace of old age would be well earned by both of them.

Then came the War.

September 7th, 1940, saw the first blitz over London, and one night a high explosive blew that city firm to bits. Warren no longer journeyed each day to work.

They were too old to begin again. What was left to them had been invested in this cottage.

They told me all this in a shy, diffident manner. Sometimes I had to guess at what they left unsaid. They talked, without pity for themselves, but full of compassion for others. When Warren spoke of smashed and mangled children being taken from a bombed building, his wife gave a little gasp. "God could not let such wicked men endure!"

They were not pretentious or clever folk. But their lives had been a pattern of goodness. Troubles had been faced with patience and resignation. Only the violence that had now entered their lives hurt and puzzled them.

How could men be so cruel?

"My boy was in the army," Mrs. Warren said, shyly; then to her husband, "Dad, perhaps Mr. Scott would like to see Dick's picture!"

Warren got out a snapshot. It showed me a young man in his twenties, curly-haired, boyish. He was in khaki, with his forage cap to the side of his head. Across his face was the confident smile of youth.

"Very nice," I murmured. "Where is he now?"

She said nothing. It was the husband who spoke. "He was at Dunkirk."

I sensed another tragedy. It was difficult to know what to say.

"He's missing. . . . He's my only child, you know."

The woman said it—very softly. Then Warren gave an unconvincing little chuckle.

"We'll see the young rascal back at the end of the War."

"A tremendous amount of the missing men must be alive," I said.

Neither of them answered. They seemed to be hesitating over something. Then the wife gave a little nod. It was a signal of assent. Her husband turned to the sideboard and took out two letters. Rather diffidently he handed them to me. Both looked well thumbed, well read.

"A pal of Dick's wrote one of them. The other's from his Commanding Officer. You might like to see them."

My heart sank. A letter from the Commanding Officer could surely mean only one thing.

I read the letter from the friend. It began, "Dear Mr. and Mrs. Warren." It mentioned the retreat to Dunkirk. They were there in time to escape, but Dick had gone back to help a wounded comrade. "If he had not gone back," ran the letter, "he would have got on board with us. But he refused to leave a friend. It was a fine thing to do. All of the lads join me in saying how brave we thought him. We are all proud to have known him."

The letter from the Commanding Officer said much the same thing in different words. Their son had been seen in a rowing boat, making for a destroyer. The rowing boat had been overturned, Germans had machine-gunned men struggling in the water. The letter ended on commending a very gallant man who went back to save a fallen comrade.

They eyed me tremulously as I read the letters. They were so very proud of him. They and Dick had given so much.

When I had finished reading, Warren said: "That pal of Dick's came to see us. It was very nice of him. He said that Dick had supported this wounded man for a long way and wouldn't leave him. But the Germans were a dirty lot to go for men in the water!"

He suddenly remembered his wife, and gave her an anxious look.

"Of course Dick got back to the beach all right. He could swim."

She said nothing.

The room seemed very quiet and still. I wondered how much belief these two really had in his survival. Must they think, in face of it all, that he was alive? Perhaps it was too hard to realize that they would never see him again.

I did not know what to say.

"He was very brave."

I gave the letters back to the wife. That gentle face was quite expressionless. But, as she took them, her hands trembled slightly. It was as though through them she could touch her son.

Warren attempted another laugh—if that mirthless sound could be so called. It was for his wife's sake.

"On the day he comes back we'll have a real do together. He was always fond of mother's cooking. I expect he'll want some decent English food by then."

"When he was a little boy he liked rabbit pie. He called it 'Bunny's Cottage.' I'll give him some of that."

* * * * *

After supper Warren and I walked into Cradstone for a drink.

As we sat in a corner, over our beer, it occurred to me that I had made insufficient comment on my companion's loss. I sensed that, though the subject hurt him it was something he wanted to talk about. He asked commendation, not for his own sake, but for his son's. It loomed so largely in his own life that he felt others could not be indifferent. But war is prodigious of sacrifice. The world forgets too soon.

"It was a very brave act of your son's, going back to help someone. You must be very proud."

"Dick was like that. He would never leave anyone who was hurt. He could have got away easily. But he wouldn't leave anyone—not to those swines."

I tried some comfort.

"I wouldn't worry too much. The Germans don't announce the names of all their prisoners."

Then Warren said, very simply, "He's dead."

His voice became gruff. He spoke in the rather shamefaced way Englishmen use when betraying any emotion. Then he lifted his head and looked at me. His face showed his naked grief. It was so lined and tired that he seemed to age before my eyes.

"I'd rather he was dead a thousand times than in the hands of those Germans. But I made out I think he's alive for mother's sake. It'd break her heart if she really knew."

* * * * *

Back at Pin Down Farm, Mrs. Warren showed me as much kindness as if I had been one of the family. "Had I enough blankets? I must say if I wanted anything."

I felt ashamed at having to deceive them.

I went off to my room, got undressed and lay on the bed with the lights out, smoking. Soon they went to their room, and the murmur of their voices sounded through the thin walls. This made me cautious. The slightest sound could be heard all over the cottage. I dare not move until they were asleep.

At a quarter past twelve, I put on my coat as a dressing-gown and crept on to the landing. The stairs creaked as I went down them, but the rest of the house was as quiet as death. In the parlour I shut the door before putting on the light.

I took the letter and another envelope from the sideboard and went into the kitchen. Here I put a kettle of water on the gas ring. When the water boiled I steamed open the envelope. Then I pulled out the slip of paper. I read the message with a feeling of disappointment: "9.4.41. St. Alb. 8.8. H.5. 21.5."

It meant nothing to me. A nasty blow after my high hopes.

Anyway, I jotted it down on a bit of paper, dried the envelope over the gas-ring, and licked the adhesive part of the empty envelope, transferring some of the gum to the envelope addressed to Bryant.

I pressed it down and, going back to the parlour, put it in the sideboard drawer. It occurred to me that the gas was still burning in the kitchen, so I went in there to turn it off.

Before returning to my room, I had another look at the message. Solving cryptographs and suchlike is not my strong point. But I stood in the kitchen trying to make something of it. My thoughts were far away as the door creaked and opened, so at first I was not conscious of the noise. Then I looked up. Mrs. Warren was standing in the doorway, watching me.

She was in a dressing gown, and on her face was a look of anxious inquiry. I nearly lost my head, a silly thing to do before this kind, gentle woman.

"Is there anything wrong, Mr. Scott?"

I pulled myself together. Some explanation was obviously necessary. If I missed Bryant at Horncastle, I did not want the Warren's account of my visit to alarm him. My eyes fell on the kettle.

"I'm so sorry I disturbed you, Mrs. Warren. But I couldn't sleep, so I came to make myself some tea. I hope you don't mind."

"Of course I don't mind. But you sit down, I'll do it."

She put me in a chair and began making tea with a practised hand. She was so quiet and gentle that it was soothing to watch her. She asked me about London. As we talked she gave me a happy little smile, as though she was conscious we were playing truant. We chatted gaily; and once when she laughed she looked up guiltily, in case the sound had wakened her husband. You could almost see there the girl she had once been.

There is a strange communion between two people awake together in a sleeping world. We talked long after the tea had become cold. And I think that for just a little while she forgot her troubles and her broken heart.

Then I made a stupid mistake.

There was an attractive mug hanging on the dresser, it looked as though it might be hand-painted; I got up and took it off the hook.

"This is a nice cup."

She looked at it. For a moment she was silent.

"It was Dick's."

I put it back and sat down again. The clock on the mantelpiece was ticking loudly. I had smashed a piece of contentment.

"I suppose you're keeping it until he comes back."

It was a trite thing to say. But I do not think that she heard me. She seemed to have slipped far away. Her thoughts had left this dimly-lit room, with its black-out curtains, and fled tremulously into the past; to a London house and a world that was peaceful, kindly and safe. I fancied she was looking down the years, fondling a baby's clothes, hearing him laugh and cry. She sighed—very gently.

Then she gave me a look that tugged at my heart strings.

Such a sad little smile.

"Dick's dead really, but I pretend he isn't—for Dad's sake."

CHAPTER X

I ARRIVED in Horncastle the next day. It proved to be a red-bricked country town in Lincolnshire, about twenty miles from the North Sea.

I was still a "traveller in insurance" and hoped to find Bryant at the Ox-Post. I had the advantage of knowing what he looked like; whereas with any luck, he would not know me from Adam. But I had to hurry, because something must be done before the 9th of April. It was now the 5th.

The Ox-Post was up the slope of the road to Lincoln, well out of Horncastle. It was a pub rather than a hotel. A white building, with creeper growing over the porch. A dark-eyed, coquettish maid-servant showed me into the parlour and got the landlord. He was a cheerful, red-faced man, with a very loud voice.

I asked him about Bryant. No doubt he had been recommended to the Ox-Post by the Warrens, as I had been. It was surprising to find that the landlord had never heard of him. This meant a hunt round Horncastle, and I thought it as well to learn something about the place. The landlord told me that there were a lot of soldiers in the town and a few evacuees.

"Jerry doesn't bomb us much. Most of his stuff goes Hull, Grimsby way. But you'll hear our bomber boys going over to blast them."

He mentioned the various places where Bryant might be staying, and, later in the day, I went out to have a look round. But there was no sign of him.

My bedroom at the Ox-Post was a substantial place, with a four-poster bed and solid, old-fashioned furniture—large stuff with no nonsense about it; an oak chest of drawers, and a wardrobe large enough to sit down in. There were flower beds in the garden, and a drain-pipe ran down the wall.

Later, I was to remember this.

It was evening, nearly dusk, and from overhead came a hum of aeroplane engines—R.A.F. machines. They were flying low, very slowly, and coming one at a time. I think they were Wellingtons. They looked like giant dragonflies droning across the sky.

The dark-eyed maid came in. She gave me a look through her long lashes, and asked if she could do the black-out.

"Do you come from London, sir?"

"Yes."

She sighed.

"I've always wanted to go there."

She stayed to chat about London, films and night clubs. She was interested in all three.

From time to time she looked at me through her lashes, a trick she must have picked up from the films. She hadn't quite got it yet, but with a little more practice she would probably be devastating among the local soldiery. It was clear that she lived in a maze of daydreams.

A bell sounded, and she reluctantly broke off the conversation. At the door, she remarked: "Nothing ever happens here, I wish it would."

Then, on the spur of the moment, I said: "If anyone should ask for me, will you let me know before you say whether I'm in or out? Sometimes there's people who you don't want to meet in the insurance business."

She smiled. "O.K. I'll give you the tip."

After dinner I went up to my room feeling that I was getting nowhere. The chances were that Bryant had not come within miles of Horncastle. I decided to have a last look round in the morning, and then clear out after lunch.

I had another go trying to read the two messages, and chain-smoked in an effort to find inspiration. I twisted the figures about, until they danced before my eyes. But they still did not make any sense.

"9.4.41. Wat. 4.4. H.5. 9½."

"9.4.41. St. Alb. 8.8. H.5. 21.5."

Finally, I gave it up. My only hope seemed to be Prestby Post Office, and that didn't look too promising. I had left London in high spirits; it had appeared then that I was on to something, but it had all petered out.

The next morning, at breakfast, someone asked where they had raided the night before—a question that has now taken the place of inquiries about the weather.

Then a last look round the town revealed no sign of Bryant; I went up to my room to pack.

I bundled my things into an attaché case I had bought, and then stood rather aimlessly at the window, having a final smoke. My room was on the corner, facing the back, and you could hear the traffic on the main Lincoln road. A car, travelling very fast, was coming from the direction of Horncastle. It pulled to a stop with a screech of brakes.

The maid came into the room as I finished the cigarette and was crushing it out on an ash-tray. She was breathing heavily, in a state of some excitement.

"There's two men downstairs asking for you!" she said.

There was a tingling feeling on my scalp. It was curious that I felt not apprehension, but excitement. My first thought was that it might be the police.

"Did they ask for me by name?"

"Yes. I got them to wait in the hall, and then told Mr. Gale."

(Gale was the landlord.)

"Did you say I was in?"

She shook her head.

"Do you want to see them?"

"I don't know who they are."

Was it the police? Perhaps it was somehow connected with Pin Down Farm. The Warrens knew me as Scott. "Wait a moment, and I'll see."

I went quickly to the door and out on to the landing. The hall-way was immediately below. There were two men there, I could just catch a glimpse of their heads. Gale, the landlord, had evidently joined them at that moment.

"We're here for Mr. Scott," said one of the men, "can you tell us if he's here?"

"I'm not sure," the landlord's voice was very loud. "What name is it?"

One of the men replied, but he had dropped his voice. I did not catch what he said.

"Inspector Cartwright! You're the police, eh? Is anything wrong?" Gale had lowered his voice, but it was still possible to hear his words.

Inspector Cartwright!

The men were talking in quiet tones, but it was possible to hear something of what they said. They were asking questions about me. Now, I have a very good ear for voices, and something about the talk puzzled me. It was not always possible to tell which of the two men was talking, but one thing was certain—neither of them sounded like Cartwright.

I strained nearer to the bannisters. The group had moved a few steps, and one of them had taken off his hat. I could now see their faces. The one dressed in a Melton coat had a broad face and big features. I recognized him at once from Warren's photograph.

It was Bryant.

The other was a small man, the fellow who had been waiting for Carr in the Kensington High Street public-house.

It was easy to guess what had happened. Bryant had gone back to Pin Down Farm. The Warrens had told him about the persistent insurance agent. He had become suspicious, pressed for a description, and here he was.

The point was, did he know that I was Michael Stephen? Or had he come merely to check up on an unknown? They had used the name of Inspector Cartwright. Did that mean they did know?

This made my position a little easier (their not being the police, I mean). No, on second thoughts, it made it worse. It depended on what move these men made. They might try and get me into the car. If I offered resistance, they would get help from Gale. It was possible that they had forged warrant cards.

It was obvious that if I insisted on the police coming in, it would be playing their game. They would like to see me arrested.

The trumps were all in their hands. These thoughts went through my head in a flash. Then I started back to my room. I was shutting the door behind me when Gale said: "Shall we go up to his room and see?"

I had just about time to find sanctuary. The girl was looking at me, wide-eyed.

"They're men I owe money to. I daren't see them!" I whispered, urgently.

The attaché case was packed. I was wearing my coat, my hat was on the bed. The hat and coat went into the wardrobe.

"Say I've gone. Here's two pounds. One for the bill and the other for yourself. Make up some story!"

I remembered that I had been smoking. There were tobacco fumes still lingering in the room. These men would notice a point like that. I gave the girl a packet of Players and a box of matches.

"Light up a cigarette and then lock me in the wardrobe. Keep the key!"

I took her acquiescence for granted. There was no time to do other than instruct her and to trust to her dramatic instinct. I stepped inside the commodious wardrobe and pulled the door shut. The next second the girl had turned the key in the lock.

There was the sound of the bedroom door opening. Then people came into the room. I stood rigid and still.

Gale said: "Where's Mr. Scott, Rosie?"

"He's gone, sir."

"When? He hasn't paid his bill!"

"He gave me this pound to give you, sir."

Then one of the men broke in impatiently.

"When did he go?"

I could sense the girl hesitating, and found myself clenching my fist. These two men would be watching her face. They would detect any obvious lie.

"He left about twenty minutes ago, sir."

I breathed again.

"Did he say where he was going?" said Bryant.

"No, sir."

"Did he say why he was going so suddenly?"

Again a short pause. It was impossible to know how clever was the girl. But I need not have worried. The male is strong, the female weak. It is nature's compensation that women can so easily fool men.

"I think he found a friend with a car who was going to give him a lift, sir. But I don't know which way they went."

She had earned her pound!

There was a short silence. It began to look as though my late quarry—now my pursuer—had been floored. Standing there in the dark wardrobe, with its faint smell of varnish, recalled to my mind a half-forgotten incident of childhood. I had been playing hide-and-seek, and had hidden in a cupboard. The "he" had come along; the squeak of approaching footsteps—

fingers touching the woodwork. How vividly I remember tingling with suppressed excitement, holding my whole body braced lest the "he" opened the door and caught me. Much the same sort of feeling came to me now. Nor did it appear that the men were quite satisfied. I held my breath again as one of them said to the girl: "Someone's been smoking in here!"

"Yes, sir. I found a packet of cigarettes and had one."

I pictured the girl taking the burning cigarette from behind her back, and giving Gale a guilty look.

"It looks as though he's gone. I'm afraid we can't do anything about it," said the landlord, loudly and decisively. "You can have a look at the register, if you like."

It seemed that my immediate trouble was over. But the next moment this happy thought was dispelled.

"We'll take a look round the room," said Bryant.

"All right, Inspector. Come on, Rosie."

My heart sank. I could not get it out of my head that the two German agents knew that I was hidden in the wardrobe. They were getting the landlord and the girl out of the room only in order to get hold of me. The bedroom door opened and shut. Presumably the two men were now by themselves.

They began to whisper. It was possible to catch only a few of their words. But the tenor of their speech was clear. They did not know what to do. They wished to continue the pursuit, but were not sure in which direction to go. Finally Bryant said: "Have a look to see if he's left anything." I heard them moving about the room. They opened the drawers of the chest of drawers, and then the handle of the wardrobe was turned. It seemed an eternity before the other man said, "It's locked."

"Never mind. Nothing here. We'll go."

Soft footsteps away from me. The bedroom door was opened and then closed again. My lungs expelled the breath joyfully from my body. The worst was over. At least, it looked like it, though I had still to get out of the hotel. Then a nasty thought occurred to me. What if the maid had become suspicious? My story had been pretty thin. She would be a fool to risk her job for the sake of a strange man.

I strained my ears for some sound, but heard nothing. Then I tried pushing at the wardrobe door. Unfortunately, it was firmly held. There was a penknife in my pocket, and I slid its blade into the crack of the door, hoping to push back the lock. But the metal would not budge.

Then the bedroom door opened.

I stood still as death. A key was inserted in the lock. A moment later I was blinking at the light.

"It's all right!" whispered the maid, almost beside herself with excitement.

"Have they gone?"

She nodded, hugging herself in a thrill of trepidation.

"Mr. Gale's downstairs. He says you must be a crook!"

"I've no time to listen to compliments. I've got to get out."

"You can't go downstairs!"

"That's true. Mr. Gale might not be deceived when I inform him I'm only your kid brother."

I went over and opened the window.

"This looks like the way."

At the end of the garden was a hedge, and beyond that—fields. If I could get safely behind the cover of that hedge I stood a good chance. It depended if anyone was about to spot me.

"Was Mr. Gale in the front of the house?"

"Yes. In the bar."

I gave her my attaché case.

Climbing down drainpipes is easy in theory, but not so simple in practice. I went down cautiously, and from the safety of the ground I held out my arms. She threw down the case.

"Good luck!" she whispered.

I walked straight down towards the hedge. I hadn't the moral courage to look behind to see if anyone was watching me. At any moment I expected a shout and the beginning of a chase.

A hole in the hedge let me through. I turned and waved at the girl standing by the open window. Then I began walking in the shelter of the hedge, away from the direction of Horncastle. I got some trees and another field between myself and the Ox-Post Hotel, and then reached the Lincoln road.

I tramped on, my mind working on the two messages. It was mortifying that I could make nothing of them, for it was clear that they must be of some importance.

April the 9th!

The date began burning itself into my brain. I felt as if I were back in an examination room at school, with a set time in which to solve a problem and no idea how to do it.

A roaring noise broke in on my reverie. A fellow on a motor bike was coming up behind me at a cracking pace. I stopped him.

"Could you give me a lift to Prestby?" I asked.

"Where's that?"

He pushed up his goggles and slipped the knapsack off his back. He was a young fellow, about seventeen, with a mop of fair hair and a grin. Together we consulted the map taken from his knapsack.

"I go through Lincoln, Saxilby, then north to Gainsborough. Where's Prestby? . . . It's not very far from where I turn towards Gainsborough. I can put you down there."

"That'll be grand."

I got on the back, clutching my attaché case, and he trod on the kick-start. While bouncing on the pillion seat I tried to do some thinking. Did Bryant know that Anthony Scott was the same person as Michael Stephen? Did he realize that I knew of the three addresses? If so, it looked as though there would be a reception committee waiting for me at Prestby Post Office.

Even in my most pessimistic moments I could not visualize squads of German spies waiting about England to trap me. But, however few of them, they had one advantage over me; they knew I could not go to the police. I was one against many.

After Lincoln we stopped at a pub for a meal.

My gaze went frequently to the window, my ears listened for the first sounds of pursuit. For now my enemies had got a feel of me; the hunt was getting warmer. I listened as the beat of each motor became audible, only relaxing when it had zoomed away into the distance.

The boy, who was going into the Air Force, asked me how old I thought he was, and when I said seventeen-something, he looked disappointed.

"A lot of people think I look older—eighteen or nineteen. I'm actually seventeen and a half." He looked at me, and continued: "You know, they don't give a pilot a very long life. I don't suppose I shall live much more than eighteen months. That means that what is a day to you is a month to me. So I haven't got much time to do things."

He was off to see a girl in Scotland, and was troubled by the attentions she got from Polish officers. Then the thought of his R.A.F. uniform cheered him up.

". . . And if she thought I was liable to be killed, she might soften a bit. I think women do, don't you? Or do you think that puts them off?"

"No. I think it'll help you. Women are apt to fancy themselves in emotional rôles."

He paused in his tragic musings to eat another scone.

"They make these damn well. I wonder if they've got some more?"

He told me he dreamt of the day he would get in the air and shoot down Germans.

"My brother is in the Tank Corps," he said, "and the silly idiot ditched his car going to Dunkirk. He said that when they were walking back, the roads were absolutely packed with refugees. Once a German plane came along and shot a lot of them. Then a woman ran past carrying a little girl. My brother shouted to her to lie down, but she was in such a terrific funk she couldn't understand. Then the German plane wheeled and came down after her. I don't think she was killed at once, because when she fell she tried to cover up the kid for protection. After the German had gone, my brother picked up the girl, who had been hit. He said she screamed like anything, but after a bit she got quieter. I don't suppose she was very old. Even when she died he still carried her."

We came out into the sunshine and remounted the motor bike. Shortly before the road to Gainsborough and the north, the boy got out his map again.

"If you go down there, you'll reach Prestby. I don't think it's very far. I'm awfully sorry I can't take you there, I'm in such a frightful hurry."

And the youngster to whom every day was a month impatiently fingered the clutch. I thanked him, and he gave a terrific grin. His motor cycle roared as he rode away. Soon he was out of sight down the white, winding road.

CHAPTER XI

As I WENT along, I felt that I was walking into trouble. It would be foolish to believe that my enemies would not consider the possibility of my turning up at Prestby. I wished now that I had taken a better look at the boy's map. A knowledge of the topography of the place would be useful.

An old man trimming the sides of the road told me that Prestby was "a tidy way." I asked him if it was a big place, and whether a town was anywhere near, because an idea was forming in my mind. He told me that it was a village, and that the nearest town was Market Bosney.

On the other side of the hedgerow lambs were frolicking in a meadow. Further on, a motor tractor was ploughing up a field, cutting chocolate lines across a sea of green, while behind wheeled a white cloud of sea-gulls. The war seemed a distant, unreal thing. I felt resentful that uncomfortable activity probably lay ahead of me.

Something like an hour's walk brought me to Market Bosney. It was just another sleepy English hamlet, with the peace of centuries stamped on its mellowed red brick. There were little houses with white doors and windows; and a tempo of life that was turgid and slow.

I took a room at the White Hart, registering in the name of H. H. Wicket (that individual's identity card still lay in my pocket). Then I smoked a couple of cigarettes in my bedroom while turning things over in my mind. Obviously I could not go to Prestby if it meant walking into Bryant and his friends. The only solution was to send someone else.

So I went downstairs and put a trunk call through to Penny. I asked her if she could come down, and she said, "All right."

"Will you bring me a coat and a trilby hat, size seven and a half? And don't forget your A.R.P. badge!"

She started asking me questions, but I shut her up. Luckily she was quick on the up-take.

"Listen, darling," I said, "don't forget that we're married and that your new name is Mrs. H. Wicket. If you come down here using your maiden name, you'll get us talked about. This is a respectable hotel."

"You sound as if you were tight!"

"Our marriage was so sudden that I haven't recovered from the shock."

"Neither have I. All right—darling. By the way, there's one thing that might help a little—if you were to tell me where you are."

"It's the White Hart, Market Bosney, near Lincoln."

"I'll be there. But I'll have to ask my boy friend first if he minds my joining my husband."

"Good. It'll give me time to get rid of the blonde. I'll see you to-morrow, then. Goodbye—darling!"

In the morning I told the landlord that my wife was coming down. He was, fortunately, a talkative man, too busy imparting information to be curious about me. I kept to my room until lunch time, and soon afterwards Penny arrived, looking cool and trim. The sight of her was like a tonic.

I kissed her, and picked up her suitcase. As we went upstairs she asked, "Why the kiss?"

"Local colour," I replied.

In the double bedroom she looked at my things.

"Is this more local colour?"

"We don't stay here to-night," I replied, primly.

Penny tossed her hat into a chair, lit a cigarette, and flopped down on the bed.

"I brought you down a hat and coat and my A.R.P. badge. By the way, why the badge?"

"Just a hunch. It might come in useful."

I told her roughly what had occurred, finishing my story by saying that there should be the letter for Pennington waiting at Prestby Post Office.

"I don't want to get it myself because there's a chance this fellow Bryant may be waiting for me."

"But if they're already at Prestby, they'll have collected the letter."

I shook my head.

"I'm not so sure about that. You see, the only explanation I can give about those letters is this—some information, or instructions, are being sent to these agents. But it looks as though they don't necessarily know each other. The chances are that they are independent cogs, so that if one is arrested he can give nothing away."

A little frown creased Penny's brow.

"Then why should Bryant know about Prestby Post Office."

"Maybe he doesn't. Or maybe he knows the address without knowing Pennington, who collects the letter."

"So what do we do?"

I gave her a smile.

"I wonder if you could go to Prestby Post Office and get the letter?"

"How far is it?"

"They tell me two miles."

"Thank you!"

"Very bracing air about here. You'll like it."

I smoked a good many cigarettes while waiting for Penny to return. Several unpleasant possibilities suggested themselves to my mind, though reason told me that not much harm could come to anyone in a rural Post Office.

I got to calculating how soon she would be back with the letter. It was two miles to Prestby. Assuming that the average person walks four miles an hour, she should return within that time. When the hour had gone by I got into quite a panic, and my heart beat like anything when the door opened to admit Penny.

She came into the room, shaking her head with a little *moue* of disappointment.

"She wouldn't give it to me. Sorry!"

"Why not?"

"It was registered. They wanted some sort of identification. And the trouble was that I had already said I was Mrs. Wicket."

What did you do?"

"I said I'd come back later with an identification card. I didn't know what else to say."

This was awkward.

I wondered why the letter was registered. Perhaps it held something vital. Suppose it contained the anti-submarine device plans? For a moment I toyed with the idea of ringing up the police, and letting them get hold of the letter. But if it only contained an apparently meaningless jumble of words, the police would consider it a hoax. It would merely mean that their visit might warn my enemies.

Penny looked questioningly at me.

"What are you going to do?"

"What is Prestby like?"

"Four cottages, four pubs, and the post office and village shop combined."

"Would the post office be easy to get into?"

"Yes, you just open the door and move forward."

"My angel—I mean to break in."

"No. It wouldn't be very hard."

I got her to describe the place. It was at one end of the village; a converted cottage, with a small garden in front. It sounded an easy place to rob, except that the woman who ran the post office kept a dog.

"Did the dog look as though it might bark?" I asked,

"It not only looked—it did."

"That's awkward. Where is the letter kept?"

"Well—first of all there's the living-room of the cottage, the other room is the shop, full of groceries and things. There's a table with weighing scales and a metal box for stamps. The letter was in a chocolate box—on the table."

We debated the advisibility of my having a shot that afternoon. I thought that if I went in for some cigarettes, it would be possible to get the old woman out of the room while I stole the letter. Penny thought "No." The postmistress had seemed a pretty shrewd old girl; and, of course, there was the risk of meeting Bryant. So it was decided to try that night, instead.

"That means we stay here for the night," said Penny. "Where do I sleep?"

"On the bed."

"And you?"

"On the floor. And if you've got anything like a heart, you'll give me one of the blankets."

We had tea downstairs. I wanted to appear in public as little as possible, but it would have aroused suspicion to have kept to our room. I had meant to tell the landlord some story about ourselves. Volunteering information often stops gossip. Fortunately, as it turned out later, we never got a chance, he was far too busy talking to us.

The lounge at the White Hart was empty, and we spent about an hour trying to unravel the letter clues. I wrote them down:

"9.4.41. Wat. 4.4. H.5. 9½."

"9.4.41. St. Alb. 8.8. H.5. 21.5."

Then we got bits of paper and tried to puzzle it out. All I could remember about codes was that the letter "e" was the one most frequently used. So we tried that. It got us nowhere. Then we jumbled the letters and numerals up; but nothing came of that either.

We knew no more than when we had started. Just the date, April the 9th, which left us less than forty-eight hours in which to do everything.

"Oh, Lord!" sighed Penny, at last; and we gave up.

The hotel bar closed at ten o'clock, and by half-past Penny and I were the only people in the lounge.

Robbing His Majesty's mails requires nerve, and I had sunk a couple of large glasses of whiskey.

I went in search of the landlord, and told him that I always walked before going to bed—because of insomnia. He expressed no surprise when he gave me the key. I suggested that it would be unnecessary for him to wait up for me.

Obviously, if my mission was successful, the stranger who strolled about the countryside at night would be an object of suspicion. But I did not mind this. Penny and I would be off first thing in the morning, long before the police began making enquiries.

I took Penny's torch, a penknife, and a steel paper-cutter from the bureau in the lounge. Penny whispered "Good luck," and just before eleven I slipped out of the front door. My footsteps sounded loud on the pavement, and soon I began walking softly, as if I were in church. With the town behind me and hedges on either side, I quickened my pace. The fields were bathed in white by the moon, and branches of trees formed a clear-cut frieze against the sky. The silence was heavy. My nerves told me that enemies were waiting behind each clump of trees; my reason told me not to be such a fool.

It was not long before I reached the hamlet of Prestby. A few brick cottages; the square tower of a church—dark against the skyline; and one or two sheds. Here all was quiet. I passed through and found, at the far end, the post office cottage. Over the trim hedge I could see a red letter-box let into the wall. It was as yet too early to make any attempt. So I went through a gate and sat in the shelter of a hedge.

As I looked out over the white patchwork of fields, merging in the middle-distance into shadows, a sudden noise startled me. I looked round sharply.

Something was moving in the shadow of the hedge, about thirty yards away. There came the distinct clink of some metal. I froze still. The noise was repeated with some regularity.

I could see nothing, for I had purposely chosen the side of the hedge that lay in the shadows. There was a piece of wooden stake by my side, and with a vague idea of using it as a weapon, I picked it up.

I began moving towards the sound. Almost at once it ceased.

When I had gone twenty yards I saw that it was a rabbit caught in a steel trap. The metal had been banging against the stump of a tree as the creature struggled to free its leg. The kindest thing would be to kill it. So I gave it a blow with the stick.

It was now a few minutes to twelve, and I decided not to wait any longer. Keeping in the shadow of the hedge and walking as silently as possible, I went back to the cottage post office. No glimmer of light appeared from behind the black-out windows.

I opened the wicket-gate and walked on tiptoe up the gravel path. The door was locked. When I slid the thin blade of the paper-knife between the cracks I discovered that it was bolted at the top, but there was no bolt below the handle. No doubt an expert could have broken in, but I couldn't, at least not without making a good deal of noise. The old woman was probably sleeping in one of the rooms above. Besides, there was the dog.

The window was a small casement affair, not large enough to get through without making the devil of a racket. So I flashed on the torch and peered through the glass. A piece of slotted metal was screwed into the woodwork and held the window in place.

I slipped in the blade of the paper-knife. It was not easy, because the slit was a narrow one, and leverage could only be exerted with difficulty. I fiddled about, sweating at the delay, but soon the thing was free. The window swung open.

By lifting myself on to the window-ledge I was able to turn the key in the door. It gave out a squeaking sound that sent my heart racing. The bolt was easier. Evidently this had been recently oiled, for it slid back without a sound. The next moment I was inside the cottage.

I can well imagine what a professional burglar must experience when breaking into a house. There was a sickening feeling in the pit of my stomach. I scarcely dared breathe. Every moment I expected the warning bark of the dog—the appearance of the postmistress. And yet despite all this, there was a curious thrill that was not unpleasant. The rays of the torch I played quickly round the room. It was small, low-ceilinged and crammed with furniture, cheap brasswork and china. Immediately to my left was another door, leading into the shop. There were groceries, tins and packets of various goods. On the table stood the weighing scales, and a metal box.

Of the vital chocolate box there was no sign.

At least, that is not quite right. There were stacks of chocolate boxes, the kind from which the contents are sold loose. I opened one of them, it contained an assortment of buttons. Then another, inside this were reels of cotton.

I began to open box after box. Picture postcards, aspirin tablets, corn cures, collar studs, pins, and a host of other articles. I felt as if I were in a nightmare, an endless dream in which I searched through box after box. And all this time, anyone passing the cottage could not fail to notice the light of my torch. I had opened every box in sight, and had not found the letter. I went through them all again, in case I had overlooked it. But in vain.

Then, I looked under the table. Women have a great faith in merely hiding something from view. Sure enough, a chocolate box was on the floor. Inside it were three letters. The one in the middle had the blue pencil marks of the registered letter. I put it in my pocket.

I went out quickly, and from the outside leant through the window, turned the key and shot the bolt. Then I shut the window. The dog did not begin to bark until I was halfway down the gravel path. Penny was right, it made the devil of a racket. I walked past the wicket-gate in an agony of mind, and down the road, accompanied by enough noise to wake up the entire population of Prestby.

I dared not hurry. If anyone looked out and saw a running man, it would be all up. I suppose the distance from the cottage post office to the end of Prestby was less than a hundred yards. But now it seemed interminable. I was just about abreast of the last cottage, when a man stepped from the shadows.

"Good evening!" he said, gruffly.

I gave a great gulp, but knew that it would be fatal to show any discomposure.

"Good evening."

I hoped that my voice sounded normal to him, and not hoarse and false as it did to me.

"You're out late."

I stopped.

"Yes. I've been sleeping badly. I thought a walk might do me good."

"Oh!"

The exclamation might have meant anything.

"Where do you come from?"

"Market Bosney."

"Quite a walk you've taken!"

He stood close to me and scrutinized me. He was a middle-aged man, powerfully built, with a round, weather-beaten face. His glance was critical and suspicious.

"That dog's making a noise!"

"I expect he heard me on the road."

"I didn't see you come through the village!"

"I've been out the other way. A rabbit was caught in a trap, and I went into the field to kill it."

"I see. . . . Are you going back to Market Bosney?"

"Yes."

"I'll come with you."

He went back into the shadows, and emerged wheeling a bicycle. I had no idea who he might be. If he was one of Bryant's crowd, he might be leading me into a trap. Perhaps it would be advisable to run for it now, while he was alone. But I thought I'd wait a bit;

attack is the best form of defence, and I said accusingly, "You're out late."

"I'm an air-raid warden."

His hand went to his pocket for a cigarette. He was wearing a raincoat, and as he pulled this back I saw the flash of an A.R.P. badge on his lapel.

He began asking me more questions. It was clear that he was suspicious about me. I told him that my name was Wicket, and that I was staying at the White Hart with my wife. When he pressed for further information, I got the conversation on to London. I spoke about the A.R.P. post in the mews off Devonshire Street as though I had been a permanent warden. I threw in all the technical stuff I knew. He thawed a little.

Soon we were on the outskirts of Market Bosney. Quite obviously he was determined to check that I was staying at the White Hart. He came with me as far as the hotel, and stood there until I had inserted the key and opened the door.

"Good-night," he said.

"Good-night."

Shutting the door, I crept upstairs to my room. Penny was in bed, asleep. I did not wake her. My fingers took out the letter and ripped it open. The message it contained was as brief as the earlier ones: "9.4.41. Barn. 5.1 H.5. 9½."

I stared at it dully. Another disappointment. I suddenly felt very tired, and wrapping myself in the blanket I fell asleep.

Penny was the first to wake. When she roused me, she was fully dressed. I showed her the message.

"That doesn't help much, does it?"

"No."

We had arranged to leave early. It was too risky hanging about. As soon as breakfast was over, I went in search of the landlord, and asked him to get hold of a car to drive us to Lincoln.

He was very loquacious. He told me about the children evacuees that had been brought to Market Bosney and Prestby. I thought it policy to conceal my impatience.

"There's been trouble with them," he said, "I'm not saying most of them aren't all right, because they are. But a lot of them come here with scabies, sores and vermin. It's not nice, coming into people's houses. I'm not blaming them, mind you. Poor little mites, it's how they've been brought up. Some of the people are very good to them. Especially a Miss Butler, she's the Billeting Officer at Prestby."

Time was getting on. I began to have visions of the postmistress at Prestby discovering her loss. Meanwhile, the landlord had discovered another topic.

"Now that they've started conscripting the women, I don't know what we're going to do. One of the girls in the kitchen is twenty. She registers on the 19th of April. We won't have any servants left!"

I reminded him that he was going to get me a car.

Then I joined Penny in the lounge. We had both done what little packing there was, and now sat waiting for the car. We did not talk much. For my part, I did not feel very cheerful; Prestby Post Office had been my last hope.

A maid came into the lounge and over to us. Presumably she was going to ask about our suitcases. Certainly I did not expect the bombshell she let fall.

"Excuse me, sir, there's a gentleman to see you."

I was too taken aback to feel alarmed.

"Did he ask for me?"

"Yes, sir. For Mr. Wicket."

"Who is he?"

"A Mr. Farraday."

Penny and I exchanged glances. My first thought was that it must be Bryant.

"What's he like?"

"He's got a policeman with him, sir."

That sounded an apt enough description.

"All right."

The maid went away.

"It's trouble! You'd better clear out," I said to Penny.

"No, I'll stay."

"I wonder if we could get out."

We looked hopefully at the window, but it was too late. At that moment Mr. Farraday walked into the lounge. He was my Warden of the night before. Behind him was a uniformed policeman.

I got to my feet. It would have to be bluff now.

"Good morning," I said.

"You'll have to excuse me," said Farraday, "but I had to report your presence to the police."

I gave them a puzzled look.

"Why's that?"

"We've got to check up on all strangers," said the policeman, rather uncomfortably.

"Oh, I see. This is my wife."

The two men nodded at Penny. I began to feel rather more hopeful. If they had come to arrest me, they would not have been so polite. They were not sure of their ground. Of course, their story about checking on strangers was stuff and nonsense. Someone had tipped them off; possibly Bryant. Or else I had aroused Farraday's suspicions by my midnight walk.

If I kept my wits about me, it might be all right. Obviously the police must have had dozens of tips about Michael Stephen. With strangers and evacuees in the place and the talk of invasion, there was bound to be a minor spy scare. The policeman did not appear to be unusually intelligent.

On the other hand, it would be fatal if they held me for any length of time. Soon I was bound to be recognized. And the theft of the letter must eventually be discovered. Right now, it seemed to be burning a hole in my pocket.

"Could I see your identity card, sir?" said the policeman.

"If I've got it." I gave a little laugh. "It's just the sort of thing you lose." I fished about in my breast pocket.

"No, here it is."

He looked at it, and then handed it back.

"Thank you, sir."

He turned to Penny.

"I suppose I ought to ask for yours, Mrs. Wicket."

Penny was splendid.

"I'm afraid I haven't got mine." She gave a laugh ringing with sincerity. "I hope you're not going to summons me."

The policeman gave a sheepish grin.

"No, mum."

The warden, who appeared to be no fool, nudged the policeman.

"I'm afraid I'll have to ask you for an explanation of your business here, sir," said the latter. "If it's satisfactory, it'll be all right."

This was a nasty one. It looked as though they might mean to hold me. Then I had an inspiration. If you tell a lie, tell a big one. It is a paradox that you can often hide something by a blaze of publicity. The landlord's recent conversation came back to me.

"I have been doing A.R.P. work," I told them, "and then I was transferred to the Ministry of Home Security. I'm down here now looking into the evacuation problem. We want to stop some of the unfortunate friction between the evacuees and their hosts."

I casually took a piece of paper from my pocket. It was blank, but I did not let them see that.

"To-day I'm calling on the billeting officer at Prestby," I appeared to consult the slip of paper. "Prestby—a Miss Butler."

That shook them all right. The grimness faded from Farraday's face. The policeman relaxed entirely. I pressed home my advantage.

"If you're not doing anything, Mr. Farraday, you could be of great assistance to me."

I think that settled it.

"I'd be glad to," he said.

The maid came in to tell us that the car was at the door, and we all went out to it. I had a nasty feeling that the landlord might appear and start talking about Lincoln. Luckily he did not do so. Nor did the driver make any comment when I told him to go to Prestby.

We all got in. It appeared that the policeman's work took him to Prestby. Possibly he felt it his duty to confirm that I really went there. During the drive, Penny chatted gaily. Her A.R.P. badge was prominently displayed in the lapel of her costume. She talked about A.R.P. to Farraday, instilling confidence with every turn of the wheel.

At Prestby we sought out Miss Butler. She was a rather intense, well-meaning spinster, wearing tweeds and a worried look. She expressed no surprise at my professed visit from the Ministry.

I had, perforce, to continue playing my new rôle. So I visited some of the cottages, incidentally, learning something of the problems of the evacuees. As one of them put it: "The trouble is not 'aving an 'ome of your own. A woman wiv'out an 'ouse is like a ship wiv'out a rudder." And a hostess said: "We're real sorry for the evacuees. They've had to leave their homes, and I know what that means. But after all's said and done, we all of us like a bit of privacy, and they spoil that for us. After all, home's home!"

When I had finished, I was a little uncertain about my next move. It was difficult to tell whether the policeman and Farraday were fully satisfied. I thought I knew a way to clinch things.

"I'd like to give the people a talk," I said. "Is there any place where I could do that?"

"There's the Methodist Chapel," said Miss Butler. "I'll see if I can get that."

Then the policeman and Farraday went off to collect people. Despite a nagging premonition of danger, I was beginning to enjoy myself.

Penny gave me a sly smile.

"What are you going to do?" she asked.

"Make a speech."

"Can you make speeches?"

"I'm just going to find out."

Miss Butler came back and said that it would be all right about the Chapel. Soon a trickling of people began to move towards this, one of whom was a large, gaunt-faced woman.

Penny nudged me.

"The postmistress!" she whispered.

With Farraday, the policeman, Miss Butler, Penny and the postmistress, I walked towards the Chapel.

Then I got a shock.

Two men were coming along the road. One of them was Bryant, the other the man in the raincoat. Our small procession moved forward with agonizing slowness. I was very conscious of the white dust on the roadway, and of the fact that one of Miss Butler's stockings was sagging on her leg. My mouth had gone suddenly dry.

I pulled the brim of my hat down over my eyes, and turned my face to talk to Farraday. I am not quite sure what I said, but evidently some of it made sense, because Farraday talked back.

It was a tricky moment. Out of the corner of my eyes I saw the man in the raincoat give us a look. I do not think that he recognized me; or, if he did, he managed to conceal the fact. My new coat and hat probably made a difference. And, anyway, he could not have seen my face.

I was worrying about Bryant more than my speech. For the trouble would start when I went outside again. I wondered resentfully why the police had not investigated these two men. Probably they had, only to find cast-iron alibis.

Inside the Chapel there was a certain amount of shuffling before everyone got into their seats. Then Miss Butler made a speech in which she introduced me, and told them that the Ministry had sent me down from London. When she finished, there was a silence. Everyone glanced expectantly at me.

I let off a lot of talk, appealing for mutual understanding and the team spirit.

When the speech came to an end, Miss Butler asked for a vote of thanks. But I was not conscious of what anyone said or did. I was too busy wondering how to get safely past those two men.

Then I had an idea.

"Look here!" I shouted above the din. "I think this calls for a bit of teamwork from my wife and myself. I noticed that there is a matinee at the cinema in Market Bosney. I'm ready to take as many children as can get into the car. What do you say?"

They gave me another clap for this, and went off to collect their children and foster-children. I stayed inside the Chapel until a shouting horde of children had been bundled into the hired Daimler. It was an old model and roomy. Then I shook hands with Miss Butler and Farraday.

"Do you think we can squeeze you in, Mr. Farraday?" I said.

"No; you're going to be full up with these kiddies. I'll walk."

With my hat well down on my head I went out to the car. It was well that I had a screen of mothers and children. For Bryant and his companion were standing in the roadway, watching the proceedings.

There were many last-minute instructions to the children, and one woman had forgotten her boy's coat. "Come on!" I breathed between clenched teeth. Then at last the Daimler moved forward. Penny waved good-bye. I did not dare look back.

We glided along the country road, with the children yelling like mad. They cheered everything, from a cow to an aeroplane.

"It's a German plane!" shouted one of them. "It's a German isn't it, mister!"

He was howled down.

"Naw, it ain't! It hasn't dropped any bombs."

One little girl was saying: "My mummy and daddy are coming to see me soon."

I said nothing. Miss Butler had told me that a high-explosive had made this child an orphan.

We disgorged the whole bunch at the White Hart. When we were alone for a moment, I told Penny about Bryant and the other man. She was concerned.

"You'd better go!" she said.

I shook my head.

"I can't leave you to face the risk."

She looked at me.

"I think these children and England are worth taking the hell of a risk for. It's more important that you get away."

I smiled wryly.

"If I wasn't a shy man, Penny, I'd make a speech of thanks to you."

"Instead of that, you can give me some money to pay the hotel bill." She smiled again. "That's a husband's privilege."

So I walked out of the White Hart Hotel, took the road towards Lincoln, and set forth to try and solve my last riddle. On the outskirts of Market Bosney I found an unattended bicycle leaning against a cottage wall. My past larcencies had not yet hardened me, and I left three pounds as payment for it.

I began pedalling along the white road. It had been fine all morning, but now rain clouds were rolling up on the horizon. Soon they came nearer, dark and threatening. They were like great billows of blue molten lead. The air became chilly, sending a shiver of apprehension through me.

I glanced back over my shoulder, and saw something that made me think. A line of men was moving down the skyline of a distant hill. Perhaps they were troops manoeuvring, possibly they were members of the Home Guard.

I had a sudden fancy that they were searching for me, and pedalled like mad for the next mile. At Lincoln I left the bicycle in the station yard and caught a train for London.

I did not know what would happen next.

CHAPTER XII

As the train left Lincoln behind us, I settled down in my corner seat, oblivious of those around me. My eyes, gazing out of the window, saw, not the countryside, but a room in Campden Hill Gardens. Carr was once more talking to Chrissa. I began searching my memory for what they had said.

Chrissa: "Will you have it by that day?" Carr: "England will have music."

Those two sentences were very clear in my mind. "Will you have it by that day?" The "day" must be April the 9th, to-morrow. Did that indicate that Carr would not receive the anti-submarine device plans until to-morrow? And "England will have music." What did that mean?

I tried to fit those two sentences into the pattern of the letters. Once more I wrote down the three messages, hoping that something would suggest itself.

"9.4.41. Wat. 4.4. H.5. 9½."

"9.4.41. St. Alb. 8.8. H.5. 21.5."

"9.4.41. Barn. 5.1. H.5. 9½."

The 9½ and the 21.5 looked as though it might refer to time. Nine-thirty p.m. on April 9th, 1941, and H.5 appeared in each message.

I tried every possible idea that came to my mind, no matter how fantastic; but nothing emerged. Soon a sort of panic seized me. Possibly I was the only man in England who could stop Carr's plans; and here I was with this unreadable message in my hands.

The loss of the Prestby letter might mean a re-arrangement of their plans. It probably depended on how important was that particular agent's work. Against that, the German mind does not improvise, it goes ahead on its set schedule.

In London I had a meal at the Corner House in Tottenham Court Road; and, afterwards, walked along Oxford Street. I was lost in thought, scarcely conscious of the effort of movement. The light was fading from the sky as I reached Marble Arch and continued along by Hyde Park. Some instinct was taking me back to Notting Hill; perhaps subconsciously I hoped to find there the answer to my problems.

I walked vaguely for a little while, then I decided to ring up Scotland Yard. Unthinkingly I had gone up the hill and past the water tower. Soon I saw a telephone box. I went inside and dialled Whitehall 1212.

When they answered I asked for Inspector Cartwright. I gave my name, expecting some sort of reaction. All the man said was, "Hold on, will you!"

A long delay, then Cartwright's voice.

"Who is that?"

I told him.

"I haven't got time to listen to practical jokes!" said the voice.

"My name is Michael Stephen!"

"Can you prove that?"

I mentioned details of my arrest (things that only I and the police could know), and finally the voice said, grudgingly, "Very well, it's you, Stephen. Are you going to give yourself up?"

"No!" I shouted, "I'm not. But take this down, I've something very important to tell you!"

"Just a moment."

There was more delay; I cursed them for their slowness and stupidity.

Then Cartwright's voice again: "Now, let's hear what you have to say."

The Inspector spoke with irritating slowness.

I gave him an account of what had happened. He took a long time to grasp it all, and kept saying, "Not quite so fast, Stephen!" Some of the things I repeated three times, and he got hopelessly muddled up over the letters and numerals of the messages.

What a fool I thought him. It was not until I had nearly finished that the truth flashed into my mind. It was I who was the fool!

The cunning fox! He was playing with me, holding me there until the police could reach me. The long delay, the irritating slowness, it had been done on purpose, police cars were closing in on me.

"That's all!" I shouted. "You must believe that it's the truth. You've probably got less than twenty-four hours in which to act."

"Mr. Stephen! Mr. Stephen!" Cartwright's voice was urgent. "I haven't quite got all that!"

But I hung up the receiver. I was out of the telephone box, the hunted feeling back with a vengeance. My one thought was to get away, to reach some place where there were people with whom I could mingle. Because here all was deserted, and the light from the cold moon was spotlighting me for the police.

I turned into another silent road, where the houses were fronted by trim little gardens. The night was very still. The only sound was that of the wind whistling by the cables of the balloon barrage, like a train running through a station.

I nearly hid in one of the short gardens, but some instinct sent me forward; I hated the idea of staying in some place whilst they closed in on me.

Then, from the road I had just left, came the sound of a car's engine, the harsh squeak of hastily applied brakes. The police!

Perhaps if I hurried it should be possible to reach the end of the road—about a hundred yards away—before they turned my corner. I cursed the moon that lit up this white prison. I cursed the silence that betrayed the sound of my running feet. Instinct rather than design kept me to the darker side of the street.

Suddenly I checked with a gasp. Another car had turned the corner in front of me. As I shrunk against a gateway, it stopped; men got out and began moving up on each pavement, flashing their torches into the gardens.

I was trapped.

For a moment I crouched in panic. Then I slipped open the gate, and bending down so as not to be seen, I went up the short pathway. With numbed fingers I felt for the bell-push. It seemed ages before a woman opened the door.

"What do you want?"

I said the first thing that came into my head.

"I'm a Warden. We're checking on people's gas masks. Can I come in?"

The door closed behind us. The woman led me into a ground floor sitting-room. Neither her tone nor manner seemed very friendly. I did not mind, Here was sanctuary.

"Shall I get my gas mask?"

"Please."

She gave me a shrewd look, and went out. Soon she returned with her gas mask.

"Here it is."

I took it, not quite certain what to do. I made a pretence of examining it, and then handed it back to her.

"Will you put it on? I want to see if it fits."

She gave me another quick look, before moving away, and putting it on. The rubber covering with its snout-like projection made her look very inhuman. I noticed that her eyes regarded me closely through the mica.

I fiddled about with it, pulling at the straps; anything to gain time. All the while I was listening for sounds of pursuit, wondering how long it would take for the men to finish searching the street. When the woman took off the gas mask, I said, "May I see it again?"

She gave it to me without a word. Never for a moment did her eyes leave my face. She seemed to be holding herself taut and tense.

I pretended to examine the gas mask again. Suddenly she said, "Aren't you holding it wrong?"

"I don't think so. Why?"

"When the Warden gave it to me, he told me not to hold it by the strap; that if you do it stretches the rubber."

"You're quite right."

I gave her a smile, but she did not respond. Then she said: "You're out rather late."

"There's a lot of people to visit."

There was a pause. My mind groped for an excuse to stay on in the house. Had she been a little more friendly, I could have started a conversation; but her cold attitude made this difficult.

Finally, I said: "Are there any other people in the house?"

"Yes."

"Would you mind asking them to come down?"

She nodded and left the room. This time the door closed behind her. With any luck—I was safe.

There was a long delay. Then the door opened.

"Thank you so much—" I began to say—and stopped.

There were three men behind the woman; one of them was the detective who had helped arrest me.

"Yes; that's him!" he said.

The woman nodded triumphantly.

"I was lucky to find you out there. But I knew he was lying; because my husband's a Warden."

One of the men touched me on the arm.

CHAPTER XIII

AT SCOTLAND YARD I was searched. Then Inspector Cartwright gave me the usual caution. Something was said about my being held "Under the Defence Act. . . . Official Secrets Act. . . . Aiding the King's Enemies. . . ."

But I was not listening. I was too busy expostulating.

"While you hold me the real man is doing what he wants. . . . At least, you might listen to me!"

Cartwright paid no heed. When the formalities had been concluded, I was left alone. Later a uniformed man asked me if I would like something to eat. I shook my head. The door clanged. It was not to open again until the morning.

For a time sleep did not come to me. I lay on that hard bed—thinking, my eyes staring into the darkness. And in my imagination passed a mental picture of all that had befallen me. Little bits of conversation; and those irrelevant things that one remembers. The last car ride with Penny was the most vivid. I began worrying about her, hoping that she was safe. . . . The maid waving to me from a window outside Horncastle. . . . The crowd sleeping in a London Underground Station. . . . But the final memory picture to each jumble of thoughts was Carr's flat. I went over it all again, searching for that elusive clue. . . .

"England has music." . . . "Will you have it by that day?" . . .

I awoke to April the 9th, 1941.

I was taken into a small room with distempered walls, a teak desk, some hard chairs and a wall clock. There was a police stenographer there and another, man. Inspector Cartwright asked me if I wanted to make a Statement.

At any rate, they were going to listen to me.

I told them what had happened. Occasionally the Inspector questioned me, but most of the time he just let me talk. Since I left Penny out of the story, sometimes I did not tell the truth. Cartwright never took his eyes off my face, and it appeared to me that he knew I lied.

Soon it was done. My statement was taken away to be typed and made ready for signature. Again I tried to remonstrate with Cartwright, but he left with the other man.

Later, they brought me back the typescript and I signed it.

I thought of Carr working his will on this vital day. This got me into a temper, and I shouted at the detectives, telling them what fools they were. They made no comment as they left the room.

They brought me lunch, but most of the time I was alone.

There was nothing to do, nothing to see save the dull contours of the room, for it was impossible to glimpse anything from the high window. The stupor of boredom and inaction overcame me. Shut away from the world, I began to think that nothing mattered any more.

It was late afternoon before the door opened again. Cartwright, the grey-haired man of my first visit, and a stranger came into the room.

The grey-haired man carried my statement in his hand. He said: "Wouldn't it be better if you told us the truth, Carr!"

This opposition was just what I needed, it goaded me into mental activity once more.

"Doesn't my statement convey anything to you?"

"That you have a lively imagination, certainly."

I threw up my hands in an impatient gesture.

"But surely you can check on what I say!"

"No doubt a great deal of it is true."

"Then you must know I'm not Carr!"

"That doesn't follow."

"Then you're a damn fool!"

"Why go on bluffing, Carr?"

"Do you realize that while you're talking to me, the real Carr is doing what he likes?"

I began to get really angry. My nerves were a bit on edge, an outburst would be a relief. However, I had enough sense to bottle up the worst of it. Shouting at this man would not help me convince him.

I leant forward.

"Look here, will you do something? Go on suspecting me, and work on the lines that you've got the right man. But will you at the same time listen to me as if I were right?"

"I am prepared to listen to anything that you have to say."

"Unfortunately, that will do no good unless you listen with an unprejudiced mind." I looked up at the clock. "It's five-twenty. I have reason to believe that at nine-thirty, to-night, something is going to happen; something that concerns Carr."

The grey-haired man sighed with disbelief. Then he said, drily, "Can you prove it?"

"I can only tell you what I know about those messages."

"Which means nothing! You admit that?"

"I've told you that I can't understand them. But I don't see why you couldn't." I looked him full in the face. "Have you tried to read them?"

He made no reply to this.

"Look!" I said, "I'm only asking you to believe for four hours. If you can read the messages, I honestly believe that you've got the solution."

I looked round at the faces of the three men. There was no show of any sympathy. Not one of those pairs of eyes looked other than cold and cynical. I suppose it was foolish of me to be exasperated. For though the truth was known to me, these three could not be expected to see it. My flight from the police could only confirm their suspicions; and my story—it might equally well be nothing but an elaborate alibi.

I made another attempt.

"Will you believe me—just for one hour? See if you can read these messages. You could have it done here—in this room." I looked at the clock. "In a few hours you may be too late."

The grey-haired man lent back and spoke to Cartwright and the other man. They held a whispered consultation. Finally, the man who questioned me said: "And if we find nothing from these messages?"

I shrugged my shoulders.

"Then I'll have shot my bolt. You can do what you like."

Again a whispered consultation. Then they left me for a little while. I began to feel hopeful, though I realized that if they agreed to endeavour to decode the messages, they did so believing that I was Carr and that possibly I did not know the contents, but was prepared to turn King's Evidence.

At last Cartwright and another man, a stranger to me, came back into the room. I suppose the newcomer was some sort of code expert.

They had the three messages written down on a sheet of paper. The second man, a small fellow with a wart on his nose, questioned me. I do not think that he fully believed what I told him.

I asked for a sheet of paper, and this was handed to me, also a pencil. Then we got to work. There was a silence, broken only by the rhythmic ticking of the clock. Nine-thirty seemed unpleasantly near.

Soon I was scarcely conscious of the presence of the others.

I began going over and over everything. Why should Carr send messages to his agents? What could he say in so few words?

This had baffled me for so long that it seemed that only a facile optimism could hope to solve it in an hour or two. But solve it I did; at least, something occurred to me.

The messages all indicated a day and a time. Surely, then the rest must indicate a place or, what was more likely—three places.

I told this theory to the others. The little man with the wart was more sympathetic than Cartwright; to him this was nothing but a routine problem.

"Might be something in that," he said.

I moved nearer to him, putting my sheet of paper down beside his.

"9.4.41. Wat. 4.4. H.5. 9½."

"9.4.41. St. Alb. 8.8. H.5. 21.5."

"9.4.41. Barn. 5.1. H.5. 9½."

"The middle bit in each one is the code of some place—perhaps a town."

Curiously enough, I felt very little excitement now that I had got—or thought I had got—the solution.

"What about H.5?" asked the little man.

"I'm not sure about that!"

He pondered for a while. Then, "I think you're only right up to a point. It's not three towns—it's one." He paused a moment. "The only explanation for H.5 is that it indicates a district."

He turned to Cartwright.

"I wonder if I could have some ordnance maps of England? And also an index of towns."

It was now seven-twenty.

Soon the maps were brought in. The code expert (I presume that is what he was) began to read through the index of towns. From time to time he consulted the messages, and jotted things down.

Finally, he said, unemotionally, "I think H.5 means Middlesex."

He began making measurements with his pencil, holding it against the scale measured on the maps. He then drew three pencilled circles on the map itself. At last he lent back. A little sigh of satisfaction escaped him.

"Do you know Stanmore?" he said.

"Out Hendon way, on the outskirts of London," said Cartwright.

"And there's a wood there!" said the little man. "These messages refer to something in that wood!"

Cartwright and I drew nearer to the speaker.

"How do you know?" we asked, simultaneously.

"It's fairly simple. Look here! . . . 'Wat.' means Watford and the 4.4. means 4.4 miles. 'St. Alb.' means St. Albans, and the mileage is 8.8. 'Barn.' is Barnet, and there you have 5.1 miles. . . . Now, if you draw three circles on the map, using each of these places as the centre of the circumference, and a radius of the scale mileage indicated in each case, you will find that the circles all intersect here— that is, the woods above Stanmore." The speaker made a mark on the map. "I should say about there!"

He beamed at us.

"The H.5 is the clue to the district, and when you know that you can guess at the abbreviations by reading the towns in that district; you can read it as I have done—that is, by looking for a district that contains all those particular abbreviations. But until you know all the towns and mileages, you cannot tell where the selected spot might be. The result is that no recipient of a message could learn or give away the place without seeing the other messages."

"But they never got the letter at Prestby Post Office," I said.

The little man shrugged his shoulders.

151 | Danger at my Heels

"Two of them would be sufficient to give one the approximate position."

I looked at the clock, and from there to Cartwright.

"It's nearly eight," I said. "Something is going to happen in Stanmore Woods at nine-thirty! . . . Will you go there?"

The Inspector said nothing to me; instead, he went away and then came back with the grey-haired man, who said, "All right!" And I knew that they were going.

I asked if I could accompany them; not unnaturally they refused. They went out. I was alone again.

Stanmore is a part of outer London that is gradually being swallowed by the encroachment of London proper. Northeast of what was once the village lie thick woods. From here, in normal times, the lights of London can be seen in the middle distance.

In my imagination I began to follow the movements of the police. They would go quickly to the waiting squad cars, and at a signal the dark automobiles would move forward. The men sat silent and grim; sometimes their fingers would feel the comforting touch of their firearms.

An alert had sounded, and the majority of people would have taken cover. It would be a grimly waiting London through which the police cars would speed. Over their heads, miles up in the sky, were enemy aircraft. And all over London A. A. gunners were predicting heights and speeds. Shrapnel was falling. . . .

I wondered what they would find in the moon-bathed woods. There were, I believe, some houses amongst the trees, locked away in their own private grounds. And in my thoughts these places became sinister. Perhaps in one of them, Carr and his agents were meeting, plotting against England.

Soon it was after nine-thirty. When zero hour had passed, the time appeared to go quicker. One way or the other the issue had been decided.

The clock ticked on—it was ten-thirty.

Then the grey-haired man came into the room.

I knew at once that it was all right. His face told me that, long before he began to apologize. They did not tell me everything. I had to imagine a great deal of what was left unsaid.

There were four police cars, and they converged on the wood from all sides. They stopped before they reached the trees. The men got out, and revolvers in hands (at least that is how I pictured it) they moved cautiously forward over the soft earth. The moonlight made visibility good, and their ears and eyes were on the alert, waiting for any suspicious sound.

The trees were motionless against the moon-lit sky; above and behind them sounded the noise of attack on London. But here in the wood all was quiet. They walked in the shadows, amongst bracken and fern. Sometimes, despite their caution, a twig snapped beneath their feet.

Soon one of the police parties found a lorry parked by the side of the road. The driver was mending a tyre, and when they approached him he gave them a "good-night."

"This would happen to me!" he said of his trouble, and dropped his spanner on the roadway with a resounding clink. "It's the second time in a month that I've had a tyre blow on me."

They asked him if he had seen any men about in the wood, and he replied no. Then they inquired about the contents of the lorry.

"Who are you?" he asked.

"The police."

"Oh, that's different. I thought you were some nosey-parkers! . . . I've got a load of scrap there."

He did not attempt to run away until the police opened up the back of the lorry. There were four men inside the vehicle, one of whom was Carr. Afterwards, an arrested confederate of the Admiralty clerk, Fergusson, confessed that the money and plans had not changed hands until that evening.

The Germans had a short-wave transmitter, and the plans of the anti-submarine device already worked out in code. . . .

"England has music." The B.B.C. were broadcasting dance music. That is what Carr had meant.

The police took them without a fight. I fancied Carr must have accepted it with a shrug and a rueful smile. While somewhere in occupied France a German waited at a receiving set for a message that never came.

CHAPTER XIV

IN JULY I received my calling-up papers. I had arranged to meet Penny for lunch, and waited in the Criterion. America was slowly waking after Roosevelt's declaration of an unlimited emergency, moving towards the World War. Germany was driving on in the east against Russia.

My thoughts drifted back to the immediate past. I had given evidence against Carr, and presumably, he was now dead. His defeat had been but one small incident in this titanic struggle.

They had not got Chrissa; at least, not as far as I knew. I pictured her as she must have been on that April day. In some hiding place, waiting. Her hands would be folded in her lap; and she would sit calm and still. Carr did not return, and soon the truth would no longer be denied. The sickening fear that she had felt so long in her heart grew and became a terrible pain. Tears for her lover would trickle down that small, calm face.

I thought of other and finer things. . . . Crowds sleeping in a London underground station, people who laughed even though they had lost everything. . . . The grin of a youngster as he rode off on his motor bike. . . . The courage of that old couple at Pin Down Farm. . . . A.R.P. workers out under a bombardment. . . . A little orphaned girl who said, "My mummy and daddy are coming soon"; the smile she gave me, and the implicit faith of youth. . . .

Surely, men and women such as these could not go down? Churchill has said that men who come after would say that this was England's finest hour. . . . I knew that, whatever happened, she had kept her honour.

Penny came and we had lunch.

Afterwards, as we came out to the sunshine of Piccadilly Circus, a wailing sound sent my eyes skywards.

Sirens were sounding over England.

THE END

Printed in Great Britain
by Amazon

34605921R00097